STOP THE WORLD

The Raiders came from space on their way to suicide at the edge of the Universe. In passing, they casually halted Earth's rotation—and the few survivors found themselves in a world without days or seasons, half in perpetual daylight, half in eternal night, bordered by the eerie twilight zones.

Now, centuries later, extinction faced mankind. One man held the key to survival—if men dared use it!

THE TWILIGHT MAN

MICHAEL MOORCOCK

"Let me assert my firm belief that the only thing
we have to fear is fear itself."
—Franklin D. Roosevelt

A BERKLEY MEDALLION BOOK
PUBLISHED BY
BERKLEY PUBLISHING CORPORATION

For Harry Harrison

© Michael Moorcock, London, 1966

Published by arrangement with the author's agent

Part of this novel is loosely based on a two-part serial "The Shores of Death" published in *New Worlds*, 1964.

BERKLEY MEDALLION EDITION, APRIL, 1970

SBN 425-01820-2

BERKLEY MEDALLION BOOKS are published by
Berkley Publishing Corporation
200 Madison Avenue
New York, N.Y. 10016

BERKLEY MEDALLION BOOKS ® TM 757,375

Printed in the United States of America

INTRODUCTION

There are two things I normally avoid writing or reading in science fiction. One is long prologues and the other is introductions by the author. As a general rule both are usually pretentious and should be unnecessary; but in this novel I found a prologue useful since it enabled me to concentrate on telling my main story, and then I felt I had to write an introduction to apologise for the prologue (and epilogue, for that matter).

This novel started life as a somewhat loosely knit and hastily written short serial in NEW WORLDS when I had just started editing the magazine and long material was hard to come by. It was a romantic, extravagant piece of work, like most of my stuff, on a kind of Faust theme (like most of my stuff) and although it got a better reception than it deserved, many readers asked "Where's the last instalment?" because the ending hadn't made the clear point it was meant to make. Others hinted—or stated bluntly—that the science wasn't all it could be, particularly the idea of clashing galaxies "exceeding the speed of light and converting to energy". They were right. I wasn't convinced by the science either. Thus, I have rewritten the novel entirely, with only a fraction of the original plot and material, using a deliberately formal style, and making quite sure, I hope, that my theme is coherent this time.

Primarily, the story is about fear and its results. The symbolism in it is not obscure and may even be a bit too obvious for some. The fear, in this case, is the fear of death and the despair that comes with it. Essentially the novel is still romantic and extravagant, but I now think the view it takes is psychologically realistic in the description of the perfect society and how it can decline rapidly once its "freedom from fear" is removed.

The manner of Adolf Hitler's rise to power in a Germany designed as a perfect democracy was not my model, though I now see that there are parallels in the novel. I am preaching no moral in the story. I am not saying that what happens to the various characters is a good thing or a bad thing: I'm simply trying to show that, in my experience, this is what would happen to them and their society when faced with the knowledge of inescapable racial death. The story divides into two halves, the first half dealing with the general effect, the second dealing with the particular effect. This theme has been handled well in two very different science fiction novels which I admire—Ballard's *The Drowned World* and Aldiss's *Greybeard*. I have made no attempt to emulate either writer, and perhaps because I have always had an active interest in idealistic politics, *The Twilight Man* is as different again.

This obsession of British writers with such themes could partly be rooted in the historical position held by Britain today. I am fairly certain that this is one of my own influences in the selection of my themes, as well as a concern with the problems of ethics and conscience in general.

As I see it, there is an observable pattern to human existence, a basic ethic, all but immutable, which obeys fixed laws. It takes the form of a never ending ritual, a great game played by the races of mankind over thousands of years, which ensures, above all, the survival of *homo sapiens,* as an entity. The rise and fall of nations and governments, the fate of individuals, are all, essentially, controlled by this survival ritual no matter what form it takes at any particular time: there is a certain freedom of action within the rules of the game and men and nations always have the choice between enlightenment and ignorance—good or evil—freedom or slavery—to a large extent. It is my belief, based not on a religious view but, I hope, a rational one, that good must therefore always triumph over evil, even if the righteous have a hard time of it in the short term; that cancers in the form of, say, naziism—cells gone wild—are always in the long run destroyed by this blind survival instinct. No single man ever saves a situation. The heroes we have are merely the men who help a situation right itself.

This does not mean I think violence inevitable, or that I think individual life and action without value, or that I think survival inevitable. I am saying that I think certain kinds of social behaviour which have no "logical" purpose are perhaps, in the long term, our most valuable traits.

Fear of death, both personal, social and racial, is our most readily observed chief survival instinct; but this fear is also what drives us most often to the brink of disaster and creates the most terrible forms of personal, social and racial insanity. Fear moulded the character of poor Adolf Hitler, fear brought him to power, fear killed the Jews, fear moved us to war against and destroy the insane Germany Hitler controlled, and fear of Hitler accelerated the invention of the Atomic Bomb we now fear—and perhaps that invention will have done more to break the cycle than we realise at this point in our history.

Fear has many causes and takes many forms. I wrote this book to try to isolate a few—and also to entertain you with a spot of melodrama. I hope you find the mixture to your taste and that you will forgive the self-indulgence I have shown in writing this introduction in the first place.

—MICHAEL MOORCOCK
April, 1956
London, England

PROLOGUE

When she told her father she was pregnant he said, "We'll have to get rid of it," but almost immediately his morbid, introverted mind was fascinated by the idea of permitting the birth; so he put his arm around his daughter's soft shoulders and murmured, "It is wrong, however, to take life, particularly when life is so scarce in this region of the world. Let us see if the child lives after birth. Let nature decide . . ."

They lived in a grotesque tower in the twilight region. Moulded several centuries before from steel and fibreglass by a neo-naturalist architect, its assymetrical lines gave it the appearance of something that had grown, living, from the ground and then atrophied. Red dust blew around it and sparse brown lichen covered its lower parts.

The tower threw a black shadow across the rock and the shadow never shifted, for the Earth had not turned on its axis since the raid from space ages before, when the space-dwelling creatures had paused with casual ease to stop the world spinning, looted what they required, and passed on in their insane, ceaseless passage through the universe.

One of the birdlike mammalian bipeds had been left behind and from him it was learned that his race was seeking the edge of the universe. When they discovered it, they would fling their ships and themselves into the oblivion of absolute lifelessness. From what could be understood of the alien's explanation, his people were driven by a racial guilt which had existed for eons. This was all mankind could learn before the alien had killed himself.

After hearing the alien creature's story, the few survivors of the raid had accepted their fate realising the comparative insignificance of their own disaster when compared with the grandiose madness of the space-dwellers.

Now the earth, with perpetual day on one side, perpetual night on the other, and a twilight and dawn region between the two, circled on around the sun.

Psychological alterations had been bound to result from the drastic environmental changes that had occurred in the different regions of the planet. The alterations had been beneficial to some and not to others. In the sparsely populated twilight region, where Valta Marca and his daughter lived in love, the inhabitants had turned in on themselves, rarely leaving their heavily-guarded towers, devoting their time to eccentric pursuits, pleasures and experiments of a dark, narcissistic nature.

Children were scarcely ever born in the twilight region, so inbred were the inhabitants. It was customary, in the event of conception, to destroy the foetus. Valta Marca's decision to let his incestuous offspring live was the decision of a man whose mental and emotional appetites had become dulled. Having convinced his daughter that she must endure her pregnancy, he waited in morbid anticipation for the birth.

In the season of the winds, in the postraid year 345, a son was born to Valta Marca and his pale daughter Betild.

It was a lonely, unlucky birth, and Betild died of it after a few months.

Strangely for a child of incest, Clovis Marca clung to his life and grew strong and healthy in time. He flourished in spite of his father's careless and disappointed attitude towards him. His father, expecting a freak of some kind, half hoping that his offspring should be a girl so that he could continue to experiment, lost interest in Clovis as the boy grew healthier and healthier. Clovis was as delicate-boned and slender as Betild and Valta, but there was a toughness about him and a will to survive that was intensified, perhaps, by the unconscious understanding of

9

the circumstances by which he had entered the world. It was this will to live, apparent since birth, that was his most remarkable characteristic.

His brain was good, his intelligence broad, and, because of his father's lack of interest in him, Clovis Marca grew into an independent, self-reliant boy. When he was twelve, his father died. Clovis burned the body, locked up the baroque tower and set off for the daylight region which, for several years, it had been his ambition to visit.

Here, Clovis Marca discovered a world absolutely different from the one he knew. The society was the nearest thing to perfection that had ever existed; vital without being violent, stable without being stagnant. This society had resulted from a number of factors, the most important being a small population served by a sophisticated technology and an equally sophisticated administrative system. The arts were alive, there was universal literacy, the philosophies flourished. To Clovis the world was paradise and he was taken into it kindly and made welcome. He quickly responded to the frank and healthy outlook of the daylight people and had soon adapted to their way of life as if he had always known it.

Only in the deep places of his mind were the dark influences of his first twelve years dormant rather than exorcised. Perhaps it was these that led to his interest in the administrative life of the daylight region so that he sought power whilst thinking he sought to serve. He began by getting elected to local committees, rose to become a member of the upper council and at last became supreme administrator, Council Chairman. He was much admired by everyone. He was respected for his understanding, his ability to take the right decisions at all times, his awareness of the processes governing both individual human life and society in general. It was agreed that he was the best Council Chairman there had ever been.

A much respected man, Clovis Marca; famous for his philosophical writings, his easy stoicism, his unselfish energy, his kindness and his wisdom. There were many to match him in most of these qualities, but none who combined them as he did. Clovis Marca was the golden man, almost the god, the darling of his world.

Clovis Marca was in his fifth year of office when the scientists announced the catastrophe.

For several generations no children had been born to the daylight people. With lifespans of up to three hundred years, people did not feel the need to reproduce very often. Those who tried and failed thought little of it. Everyone assumed that the reason for the lack of children was because everyone else had decided not to have any.

Then a couple complained. Other couples complained. It was discovered that a large section of the population had indeed tried to have children and had failed.

Urgent experiments and tests were made.

Physics and biology were fields in which little new research had been done for at least two hundred years; it was felt that there was no need for any more information than was available to assure comfortable living.

The climate of the times had not produced anyone sufficiently interested in the two disciplines to do new research. The increase of harmless omega radiation had been measured and noted in the previous century. It was believed that the radiation was a by-product of the mysterious energies which the space-dwellers had used to stop the world spinning. The radiation had seemed, in fact, beneficial to many plants. It had produced the flower forests, it destroyed weeds, it appeared to contribute to people's youthfulness.

The tests showed that it also affected semen and ovum.

In short, it had made every man and woman on daylight Earth barren.

This was not at first thought particularly disastrous. Expeditions were sent to the twilight regions to seek people who could still reproduce.

But, whether or not they had resisted the effect of the omega radiation, the denizens of the twilight regions had inbred to the state of impotence. Valta Marca had been the last father. Clovis Marca the last child of the twilight.

A few expeditions were made by robot machines into the cold nightlands, but there, as was already known, nothing lived.

In space, then?

A thousand years before, at great expense and at the cost of many lives, Mars and Ganymede had been transformed into facsimiles of Earth. They were lush worlds and they had supplied food and minerals to Earth when they had been needed. After the raid from space, they had lost their usefulness, for the population had greatly decreased. Now only a few people existed on either planet, simply to ensure that they continued to produce food and minerals in case they were ever needed. The wardens of Mars and Ganymede and their small staffs were replaced every three months because three months was almost the maximum time that men could live away from Earth and remain sane.

It was because of this that space-travel to distant solar systems had been discontinued not long after man had first gone into space; it had been discovered that in spite of their ability to reproduce exactly Earth atmosphere and other conditions on ship or, as in the case of Mars and Ganymede, even on planets, somehow men could not bear being away from Earth for long.

There were psychological explanations, physiological explanations, semi-mystical explanations for this being so, but the fact remained: Men who were on average away from Earth for little over three months went mad with pain and a terror that welled up from the recesses of their minds and could not be controlled. Even in space, on the journey to Mars, men had to undergo the *space ache*. The word had been coined to describe the indescribable experience of leaving the mother planet. Space ache—a combination of mental and physical agony—came soon after your ship had passed the half-way point on the journey to Mars. It was possible by complicated methods, to relieve the space ache, but not to avert it.

Thus the faint hope that those men who guarded Earth's colonies for a few months every year would not have received as much omega radiation as those who had never left Earth.

It was proved that they had, while on Earth, received more than enough radiation.

There was a legend—a mere fiction, everyone knew—that a colony had been founded on Titan soon after the raid and that the colonists had managed to adapt, losing something of their humanity in the process. Half-human or not, their seed could be used.

It was an illustration of the point of desperation reached that a volunteer expedition was sent to Titan and did not return.

There was no escape from the truth after that. The space-dwellers had, probably without realising it, effectively destroyed the human race. In two hundred years everyone would be dead. Two hundred years was the life expectancy of the youngest person on Earth. Her name was Fastina Cahmin.

When the realisation dawned that the mortality of the race could not be averted a new mood swept through the society of daylight Earth. The people gave themselves up to pleasure-seeking, and a party began. It was a kind of Wake; a premature Wake held by the soon to be deceased. Too sophisticated to let it control them as yet, the people of the daylight suppressed their hysteria or gave vent to it harmlessly, in their arts and pleasures.

Clovis Marca resigned his Chairmanship of the Council and mysteriously disappeared.

The shock of realising he was never to propagate himself had re-awakened the dormant elements in Marca's psyche.

He became wholly driven by what had caused him to survive his birth and early childhood so successfully. He became wholly driven by his intense will to live.

The long party continued and the signs of the suppressed hysteria began to show—in the fashions, art and in the topics of conversation. From time to time people wondered where Clovis Marca had gone and why he had gone, though it had not taken them long to get used to instances of irrational actions by men once thought completely adjusted. It had been surprising, though, that Clovis Marca, their demigod, should break so soon—unless he was seeking still for a remedy for their plight. They told themselves that this must be so. It was comfort-

13

ing to know that Marca was making this sacrifice, even though it was absolutely certain that no hope was left.

Clovis Marca was gone a year and then he returned to his friends and his people.

They celebrated his home-coming with a party. It was really just part of the ever-present party. It was more elaborate than usual, that was all.

BOOK ONE

CHAPTER ONE

Something to Fear.

It was a noisy party, a colourful party, a splendid, exciting party, and it swirled all around him in the huge hall. It was packed full of life; full of heads and genitals and bellies and breasts, legs and chests and arms and hands; people with pumping hearts under their ribs, rushing blood in their veins, nerves at work, muscles moving. Most of their costumes were colourful and picturesque, though here and there stood a dark-clad sexless individual in heavy clothes, wearing a mask and with its head shaven. But most of them drank down the liquor and ate up the food and they danced and flirted and they talked all the time. It is necessary, he thought.

The walls of the hall were of pseudo-quartz, translucent and coloured like writhing rainbows. Pillars, arches and galleries, rising from the floor, were of the same subtle manufacture. Music filled all parts of the hall and there was laughter, excited voices. The throng seemed in good humour.

He tried to relax and join in the pleasure. A roboid waiter, human-like but running on hidden casters, paused with a tray of drinks. Clovis Marca reached out from his seat in the corner and took a wineglass; but as he did so he saw his pursuer again. The enigmatic face was in shadow and the dark clothes merged with the blackness, but Marca recognised the awkward way in which the man held his head, as if he had weak neck muscles and was keeping the head erect by an effort. Marca stared at him, but there was no response from the dark figure, no sign that he knew Marca was looking at him.

Marca sipped his drink, wondering whether to ignore the man or cross the hall and confront him. But he felt afraid.

To succumb to the fear would be irrational, he realised. Fear could be understood and controlled. There seemed no reason to be afraid of the mysterious figure. Marca frowned and stood up, stepping down from the little dais and joining the heaving, almost solid mass of people on the floor. Being very tall, he could look over their heads and keep his attention on the still figure of the man who stood in the shadow on the far side of the hall.

Almost involuntarily, Marca began to move forward. Everything but himself and the other figure seemed unreal. He was hardly aware of the warm bodies pressing against his and now even the noise of the party seemed distant.

He had held off confronting this man for too long. He had had opportunities on Mars and Ganymede to speak to him face to face. He had seen him more than once on Earth, too; but he had given in, every time, to his irrational reluctance to admit that the man existed, or that his constant presence near him was anything more than coincidence.

He knew the man only as Mr. Take. He had discovered that much from the passenger list of the ship they had both taken to Mars. The outdated form of address the man chose to use before his name was another unusual thing about him, smacking of the pointless eccentricities of the twilight people. It was even likely that Mr. Take was not his real name.

Repressing his fear, Marca moved rapidly towards Take.

Overhead a fat man levitated, laughing in a way that had not been heard a year ago. The laughter was brittle, hysterical. The fat man ascended erratically towards the nearest gallery where similarly laughing men and women reached out, trying to grab him. He was giggling so much himself that he could hardly control his flight, threatening to crash on the heads of the crowd below. He had a bottle in his hand and, as he veered about in the air like a gigantic, drunken bumble bee, the bottle spilled its contents, raining golden wine down into the hall. Some of it caught Marca in the eyes. He paused to wipe his face, and, when he looked at the corner again, Mr. Take had gone.

Carefully scanning the hall, Marca saw Take moving slowly towards one of the big oval entrances. The crowd, like the foaming wake of a ship, seemed to divide about him as he walked.

Marca shrugged. He felt relieved that the man was leaving.

Then Take turned. He still held his head in that strange way, but now he looked directly at Clovis Marca. Take's frame was thin; his head was long and pale, his sombre eyes hooded, colourless.

Marca shrugged again, emphatically, and felt someone touch his hand. It was his old friend, Narvo Velusi, the man who had chosen to protect him when, over twenty years before, he had first come to daylight Earth. Narvo Velusi was two hundred and ninety years old; a man nearing death. There were few signs of this on Velusi's face. The flesh was old, but firm, the blue eyes alert and the hair dark. He had a square face and a bulky, wide-shouldered body. When he spoke his tone was mild but vibrant.

"Are you enjoying the party, Clovis?"

Clovis felt slightly offended by the presence of the hand on his arm. He took a step back. He had never considered Velusi's age before, but now he did and the thought was unpleasant. He controlled himself and smiled.

"Wonderful, Narvo. It was good of you . . ."

"You don't look happy, though. Perhaps I was thoughtless? I should have given you time to rest before I suggested the party. After all, you only got back this afternoon . . ."

"No, I meant it. It's a relief to be back here and a
17

pleasure to be with so many people." He looked for Take, but the dark man had gone. "Did you invite a person who calls himself Mr. Take?"

Velusi shook his head. "Did you hope to meet him? He could be here. It's open house—to welcome you back."

"No—he was here. He's gone."

"I still think you seem ill at ease, Clovis."

Marca tried to smile again. "I suppose I am a little tired. I'll stay though. It would be ungracious to leave so soon."

"Not at all. Let's go. Your house has been prepared for you. If you—"

"No. I'll stay. Have you heard of this Mr. Take? A strange man." Marca described him.

"He sounds it. I should know a man like that—but I don't. Why are you so interested in him?"

"I've seen him before. Not just on Earth—on Mars and Ganymede, too. He seems to have been following me."

Velusi pursed his lips. Marca knew that he was too polite to ask him directly where he had been and why he had been gone so long. Velusi was evidently hoping to hear more. Marca was half-ashamed of himself for being so secretive with his old friend, but he had long ago made up his mind to share his ideas with no one else.

"We can find out who and where this Take is tomorrow," Velusi said with a smile. Once again he took Marca's arm. Once again Marca felt a trace of revulsion at the touch but let Velusi steer him towards the nearest gravishute. "Come on, Clovis, cheer up. Let's go and meet some friends. I think you know most of them."

Marca made himself relax as Velusi stood aside to let him enter the gravishute entrance. The gravishute was a circular shaft going from top to bottom of the house. At its base was a force-beam generator. A single button by the entrance could control the strength of the beam so that one could drift gently down or be pushed gently up. Inside the opening was a simple hand-grip which could be grasped to halt one's progress.

The harnessing of this power had contributed a great deal to Earth's present civilisation, and all techniques

18

were now based on it, as earlier they had been based on nuclear energy.

They drifted up to the highest gallery, several hundred feet above the floor of the hall. There were only a few people here, lying on couches, talking quietly. Most of them were old acquaintances. Marca greeted them politely. He sat down on a couch beside Velusi.

Several of the men and women there were ex-officials of the Council. Since the disaster, most people had followed Marca's example and resigned their jobs so that now only a skeleton staff looked after the administration. It was all that was needed.

Marca was surprised to see Brand Calax, Warden of Ganymede, in conversation with Andros Almer, ex-Controller of Public Communications. Calax should have been in the middle of his three-month duty on Ganymede. Why was he here?

Miona Pelva, a red-headed woman running to fat, smiled at Marca. She had been Deputy Chairman under his chairmanship. She had not been fat then. She was not the only person who had let herself go since last year's news.

"How was space?" She was as eager as Velusi to hear him answer the questions they had all been asking about him.

"Awful," he smiled.

"Isn't it always? Any after effects of the space ache?" She shook her head in sympathy, her floppy purple head-dress waving. "A *year* away! Was it all spent in space?"

"Not all."

"Somebody said they thought you'd gone back to the twilight region for a while." The speaker was a sharp-featured man wearing a golden gauze mask over his upper face. The fashion of wearing masks had grown up since Marca had left. Symptomatic of the suppressed hysteria now dominating daylight Earth, Marca thought.

"Really?" said Marca, thinking that people's manners also seemed to have declined in the year.

Velusi changed the subject. "Have you been to see Carleon's new novel, Quiro?" he asked the man in the

19

golden mask. "You must see it, Clovis. The mood mobiles are very impressive."

Marca felt more comfortable as the conversation went on to more general topics. A little later he rose and went over to speak to Brand Calax and Andros Almer. The men seemed to be arguing quite fiercely but broke off as he greeted them.

"Sit down, Clovis," Almer said cheerfully. "The Council's gone to pieces since you left—but I suppose there's no need for it any more. Brand and I were discussing this idea of his about sending another expedition to Titan. Do you think it's a good idea?"

Marca shrugged. "I doubt if it would achieve anything but a few more deaths. Besides, who'd volunteer now?"

Brand Calax was a squat man with a pointed, black beard. He wore an orange turban, a red, knee-length coat, open at the neck and flared at the waist, and low-heeled boots. Some said he had been born in space. Certainly he had a stronger resistance to the space ache than anyone else.

"I would," Calax said. "I could take it—I doubt if anyone else could."

"It's a long journey," Marca said.

Andros Almer scowled. He had a dark, tanned face, slightly slanting eyes and cheekbones, full lips and a supercilious expression that always seemed a little studied. "A pointless journey," he said.

"You agree we should not give up," Calax growled. "What else is there to do?"

"Anything would be better than risking your life or your sanity in a voyage through space to a planet that is barely habitable in search of a group of people *thought* to have gone there just after the raid and who would probably be dead if they had!" Almer drew a deep breath and was going to continue when Brand Calax broke in.

"I told you I had found evidence that a large expedition did land on Titan. I circled the world myself. I saw the remains of ships. I saw suggestions that attempts had been made to begin a settlement of some kind."

"You saw these things from a great distance!" Almer

20

said. "You brought back no proof that you actually saw ships and buildings. Your eyes might have deceived you. Maybe you saw what you hoped to see! Why didn't you land?"

Marca listened intently to the two men.

"Because I had little fuel left and because the space ache was getting me," Calax said sharply. "I was in a converted ferry. They haven't a big range!"

"And that's the only survey you made." Almer spread his hands. "Flimsy evidence, surely? Yet you came back to Earth to ask for a special ship to be built so that you can bring some of these 'survivors' back to Earth. Even if there were ships and buildings—do you think anyone could have lasted on a world like Titan?"

"It's possible," Calax said. "I spent nine months at a stretch away from Earth once."

"Nine months—and you're scarcely typical of the rest of us. These people are supposed to have been on Titan for four hundred years!"

Calax turned to Clovis Marca. "It's just possible, isn't it, Clovis?"

Marca shook his head. "Not likely, though. You want to build a ship, eh, to take you to Titan and bring back the people you think are there?"

"The descendants of the original expedition," Calax said brusquely. "It's a chance worth taking, I think. If I hadn't been away when the first expedition was made, I'd have volunteered. I could have made it."

"Possibly," said Almer. "I still think we should be concentrating on something more positive—creating semen and ovum artificially, for instance."

"It's been tried. Not one of our scientists has got anywhere." Calax helped himself to wine.

Marca sensed that a genuine dislike existed between the two. There seemed no reason for it. There seemed to be no argument, either. If Calax wanted to go to Titan, surely that was his risk?

He started to say as much when suddenly they all looked up. The hubbub of the party, which had been in the background all the time, had cut off sharply.

21

Marca moved to the edge of the gallery and leant over the invisible force-rail.

People were streaming rapidly from the hall. All the other galleries had been cleared. Through every exit, people hurried silently. They seemed tense.

Then they had gone and the hall was still and silent.

There was party litter everywhere and the light breeze from the entrances stirred it. That was the only movement.

Almost in the centre of the hall, near a couch, Marca saw a dark shape on the floor. It was the figure of a man.

As Almer, Calax, Velusi and the others reached the rail, Marca turned and made for the gravishute. He descended rapidly, crossed the hall to where the figure lay.

The man was dressed in the high fashion of the moment, his head shaved, his rust-coloured mask obscuring his entire face, his long, belted coat of deep blue spread out around him on the floor.

Marca knelt beside him and felt his pulse.

He was dead.

Velusi and Almer crossed the hall towards him.

"What's the matter with him?" Almer asked.

"Dead," said Marca. He peeled off the mask. The man was old. Evidently he had died of a heart attack probably brought on by the excitement of the party.

Velusi turned away, clearing his throat. Almer looked embarrassed.

"Why did they all just leave like that?" Marca asked. "So suddenly—not trying to help him or anything . . ."

"They probably decided to carry on with the party somewhere else," Velusi said. "That's what usually happens—they go on somewhere else . . ."

"I don't understand," Marca said. "You mean they just leave a corpse where it lies?"

"Usually," said Almer. "You can't blame them, can you?"

"I can't understand them, either!" Marca said disapprovingly. "What's happening here nowadays, Andros?"

"Can't you guess?" said Velusi quietly. "Are you sure you can't understand them, Clovis?"

22

CHAPTER TWO

Someone to Love

Fastina Cahmin had waited a year for Clovis Marca to return, but on the day of his arrival she had been asleep. She could go without sleep for extraordinarily long periods and could spend an equally long time catching up on it. She woke, after three days asleep, to learn that Marca had come home. Andros Almer had told her in a letter he had left while she slept.

Fastina Cahmin was a widow whose husband had been one of the Titan expedition volunteers. She was twenty-eight and the youngest woman in the world. She was the last child of the day side of the Earth as Clovis Marca was the last child of the twilight region.

She was tall, with a slender, full-breasted figure and golden skin. Her hair was black and her eyes were a deep, luminous blue. She had a small, oval face and a wide mouth. Perhaps because her lifespan would be so long, she took a genuinely sensual pleasure in living that was nowadays rare.

Before her husband's death, she had known Clovis Marca only socially, but she had been completely in love with him for several years. Her husband had loved her with similar singlemindedness and she believed, without remorse, that it was because he had realised her own obsession that he had volunteered for the Titan expedition.

She read Almer's letter.

Fastina,

My selflessness knows no bounds. We heard today that Marca is on the Mars ship and should arrive this afternoon. Remember what you told me, I hope you are unlucky.

With love,
Andros

She smiled affectionately. She liked Andros. He had been the one who had brought the news of her husband's presumed death. At the same time, knowing what her feelings had been towards her husband, he suggested that she should come and live with him. She had refused, telling him that she would first propose to Clovis. If he rejected her, which was likely, she would then accept Andros. That was what the letter was about.

She put the letter on the table beside her bed and touched a stud on the control panel. The wall shimmered and became transparent. It was a fine day. The sun, at permanent zenith, shone down on the sea. The tideless expanse of water was completely still and blue. The white beach that led up to her house was deserted, as it almost always was. In daylight Earth, people lived far apart. Their houses were self-sufficient and transport swift. There was no need for cities. The nearest thing to a city had been the few buildings which had housed the administrative offices.

Fastina lived in an area that had once been Greece, although there were no artificial boundaries of that sort any more. The planet's real boundaries were now formed by the twilight region.

She contacted Central Information on her laser-screen and asked: "Where is Clovis Marca at this moment?"

The screen replied.

"He was last observed half-an-hour ago entering the South Western flower forest."

Fastina put on her best dress. Its crimson fabric was virtually weightless and drifted around her like a cloud of blood. She took the gravishute to the roof of her house.

There her air carriage waited. Its golden body had been moulded to the shape of a fantastic bird with spreading wings. There was a cavity in the back, lined with deep red cushions. Up to four people could rest in it in comfort.

She climbed into the carriage and put a small, ultrasonic whistle to her lips. She blew a particular signal and the air carriage drifted upwards over the beach and the sea. Like a fabulous creature it swept gracefully towards the south west and the flower forest.

A little while later she walked through the flower forest, hoping that she might bump into Clovis Marca. She walked with a long, easy stride, smiling as she breathed in the scents of the huge blooms hanging above her and around her.

Everywhere rose the shining green and brown trunks of the flowers and the scents were so heavy that they drugged her into a state of pleasant lightheadedness. She looked up at the leaves, the petals, the heat-hazy sky and the sun. Beneath her feet were petals of all colours; large petals of pale purple, small ones of dark purple, pink, pale yellow and mauve. There were petals of heavy yellow, scarlet, cerise and crimson, petals of soft blue and orange, sometimes ankle deep. And there was every shade of sunlit green, from near-black to near-white, where flower trees stood tall and cool or clustered to the ground.

She turned down a path that was thick with the cerise flowers fallen from the trees above her. It was cooler in this avenue and, although like all her people she had become used to the great heat of her world, she appreciated the shade.

She did not, as she had hoped, bump into Clovis Marca. She bumped into Andros Almer instead and knew at once that it was not accidental. Obviously he had guessed she would come here.

Almer had succumbed to fashion, it seemed. He was wearing a gauze mask that gave his face a blue tinge. He wore a deep blue pleated shirt, black, tight trousers and a loose, black cloak that was gathered in at the waist and belted. He paused, bent and picked up one of the fallen cerise flowers, offering it to her with a smile.

25

She smiled back and accepted it. "Hello, Andros. Have you seen Clovis?"

"Ah," he said lightly. "If I were vain, I'd be so offended . . ."

She laughed. "I hope you are vain, Andros. Didn't Alodios write 'Vanity makes for variety in a man, whereas humility offers only the humdrum'? I'd hate you to be humdrum."

"You hate me anyway," he said with a mock frown. "Besides, if what you say is the truth then Clovis should not attract you, for his lack of vanity is well known. He's a perfect man—all virtue and no vice—a whole man. A whole man offers no surprises, Fastina. Change your mind or risk his acceptance. He would *bore* you to death!"

"I see you're not completely given over to the fashion," she said lightly. "You can still force yourself to say the word . . ."

"Death is all I want if you won't have me, Fastina."

"Don't die, Andros. It would embarrass all those poor people. After all, it's our duty to stay alive, isn't it? Just in case."

"Just in case there's a miracle and the world starts spinning and jostles our genes so that overnight we all find ourselves parents of triplets?" Andros laughed, but now his laughter was sharper. "That's the soundest hope, you know. There are wilder ones about. Brand Calax believes there are people on Titan just throbbing with healthy seeds. The only trouble is the gravity's a bit heavy and they look like walking pancakes. The big bangers might have a better idea—they want to go out in one mighty explosion. They seriously suggested we make a bomb big enough to blow up every human artifact in the world."

"Why blow them up?"

"They think they've no right to exist. They've gone off sex as well—no love-making without progeny, they say. What a syndrome!"

"Poor things. I'd never have thought people could change so much."

"It's fear," he said. "And they've got every right to be afraid. You're lucky—you don't seem to worry at all."

"I'm worried, of course, but I can't believe it altogether."

"You should have been on the Council when we gradually realised the whole truth. You'd believe it." He pulled at his dark clothes, fingered his mask. "Look at all this—I *like* the fashion, but you can see what's creating it. I must be as scared as anyone else. I haven't started shaving my head, yet, or wearing those sweltering black masks and robes—but don't be surprised if I get to like the idea in a few months."

"Oh, Andros, you're too intelligent to go that far!" She smiled.

"Intelligence has very little to do with it. Can I take you to the meeting?"

"Is there a meeting?"

"Is there a meeting! Your senses must be more distracted than I guessed. That's why Clovis is here. Everyone interested is in the Great Glade discussing Brand Calax's idea. It'll be decided today whether to let him have the materials to build his ship or not. I hope they laugh him out of the glade!" The last sentence was spoken with such vehemence that she glanced at him in surprise. *Was* Andros becoming unbalanced? She could hardly believe it.

"When does the debate start?" she asked, taking his arm gingerly.

"It's already started. Come on, we'll go there now." He put the ultrasonic whistle to his lips and shortly afterwards his carriage moved down through the flower trees hardly disturbing a leaf. It hovered a foot above the ground, its ornate metal scroll-work glistening red and yellow. Andros helped her on to the plush cushions and lay down on the couch opposite her. He blew on the instrument and the carriage rose into the hot sky. Through its transparent floor, she saw the mass of brightly coloured flowers, some measuring twenty feet across, moving swiftly past.

She said nothing as they flew along and Andros seemed to respect her silence and stared with apparent interest at the flowers until the carriage had found a space for itself among the hundreds of other carriages hovering above the Great Glade where that part of Earth's society sufficiently

27

concerned with the problem of a second Titan flight had met to debate. For a moment she thought she saw Andros glance at her in a peculiar way, but she dismissed the idea, guessing that it came from her own abnormal mental state.

"I see you're not wearing a gravstrap," Andros said, reaching under the couch. He handed her the thin, tubular belt and fitted a similar one under his arms. She did the same, clipping the thing together over her breastbone. They left the carriage and drifted down among the packed tiers until they found two vacant chairs and seated themselves.

Below them on the central dais, Brand Calax was speaking. He still wore his turban and red coat.

She did not listen closely to Brand Calax until she was sure Marca was there. He was sitting with his arms folded, dressed in a simple high-collared white shirt, black trousers and with small, dark lenses over his eyes to protect them. From his seat in the first tier, he seemed to be listening intently to Calax. Beside Clovis sat old Narvo Velusi, dressed soberly in a russet toga, his high-heeled black boots stretched out before him, his body bent forward slightly. His square, heavy face was turned towards Calax.

Calax's voice seemed harsh to Fastina. He was speaking urgently and bluntly.

"In about two hundred years there won't be any of us left in the world. The human race will be nothing but a few bones and a few buildings. Surely it's better to keep trying to stop that happening? Everyone on Earth seems to have drawn in on himself—there's an apathy I never expected to see. Do you want to die? From what I've seen in the past few days, that's the last thing you wish. Besides—I'm only saying I want to risk my own life on Titan. I know what the gravity's like and I know that that combined with space ache is too much for the average man to take for more than a day or so. But I'm used to space—I can even live with the space ache for longer than I'd need to stay on Titan, just to make sure there isn't any hope there. I'm asking for materials we'll never need to use for anything else. What's the matter with everyone?

Why don't you just let me go ahead? I'm the only one who might be hurt!" Calax wiped his forehead and waited for the response. None came. "We've got to go on trying," he said. "It's a valuable human trait to go on trying. We survived the raid. We can survive this."

"This is the aftermath of the raid," said Almer from the audience. The silvery phonoplates hanging in the air around the auditorium picked up his words and amplified them for the others. "We only *thought* we'd survived it."

Narvo Velusi got up and looked at the mediator who sat on the dais behind Calax. The mediator was a fairhaired man with a blond moustache which he kept stroking. He nodded and Velusi walked onto the dais as Calax left it.

"I think I can tell Brand Calax why we are reluctant to grant him the resources to build his ship," said Velusi quietly. "It is because we have now become so fearful that we are even afraid to hope. We are rational people normally—our society is still probably the most perfect in history. Yet we can all sense it going sour on us—our reason doesn't seem to be helping any more. I think this is because, though we know why we are behaving unreasonably, what has happened to us is bigger than reason. It strikes at our deep psychic drives—our animal drives, for that matter. We are no longer immortal as a race. We had always assumed we would be. We are beginning to behave irrationally, and I think this will get worse, no matter what we do to try to stop it. I feel that Brand Calax should be allowed to do as he thinks fit—but I share the general opinion that he will be doing it for nothing."

Velusi's calm, slow words seemed to impress his listeners. Fastina saw people nodding agreement with him. She, too, sensed his sanity, his understanding of the situation they were all in.

Someone else spoke from the audience.

"May we hear what Clovis Marca thinks?"

Velusi glanced at Marca.

Marca remained seated. He said: "I can add nothing more to what Narvo Velusi has said. I am sorry."

29

People looked disappointed. Evidently the rumour that Marca had been seeking some solution had been wrong.

Velusi continued:

"There is little hope. It would be stupid to hope. If our destiny is to die, let us try to do it well."

A woman laughed shrilly. They saw her rising towards her air carriage on her gravstrap. A few others followed her. A group of faceless, sexless people in their masks and dark clothes also returned to their air carriages. The vehicles wheeled away through the bright, hot sky.

Brand Calax jumped back on to the dais. "And let's do it fighting! Will you give me my spaceship?"

The mediator stopped stroking his moustache and got up. "Who agrees?" he asked the crowd.

Hands rose. The mediator counted them.

"Who disagrees?"

Fastina watched Andros raise his hand.

The mediator counted again.

"Brand Calax, the resources you need are at your disposal," said the mediator formally.

Calax nodded his thanks, touched his gravstrap and rose into the air.

Fastina saw Clovis Marca stand up, obviously preparing to leave. He was pointing into the air, towards a white air carriage hovering above him. Narvo Velusi was nodding. They were obviously deciding to travel in that carriage.

Impulsively she touched the control of her gravstrap and was lifted upwards, guiding herself gently towards the white carriage.

Andors shouted after her, but he did not follow.

She reached the carriage before Marca and Velusi. She drifted over the side and sat down on one of the couches.

Clovis was not the first man she had confronted with a proposal of marriage, but her heart was beating rapidly as he and Velusi reached the craft and saw her sitting there.

Clovis recognised her and smiled. "Hello, Fastina."

"Hello, Clovis. Welcome back. How are you feeling after your mysterious travels?"

"He's better today," Velusi said, settling on to a couch

and raising a whistle to his lips, "you should have seen him yesterday, Fastina!"

Marca did feel better that morning, having slept well during the period they still called 'night.' He felt more his old self. He sat down next to Fastina and kissed her lightly on the forehead. They had never been lovers, but she had always flirted with him and he had always responded cheerfully.

Before he blew the appropriate signal, Velusi asked: "Do you want a lift, Fastina?"

"Not really," she said. "I came to see Clovis. If you're busy, I'll wait . . ."

"That's all right," Marca told her. "It's nice to see you again. Come and have some lunch at my house."

She looked at him, wondering how deep his affection was. She could tell that he was attracted to her, but she knew he was not the man to begin a casual love affair on the strength of a mild attraction.

The carriage was moving away from the flower forest, passing over the occasional house. Now that there was no need for towns, public services were maintained by a big underground computerised network. The houses were mobile and a man and his friends or family could land their buildings in the scenery of their choice. Marca's house was situated at the moment close to the lake that had once been known as Lake Tanganyika. Europe, Africa, the Middle East, India and parts of Russia faced the sun, as did a tiny part of the South American continent. Most of South America, all of North America, nearly all of China, and all of Japan and the Australias, lay in the night region. The habitable world was, in fact, what had been the known world before the great explorations of the Renaissance.

Soon they could see the lake ahead, like a sheet of blue steel flanked by hills and forests. Herds of animals grazed below. While the human race had decreased, the animals had proliferated: perhaps because their life cycles were shorter, they had adapted to the omega radiation in time. It was ironic, thought Marca as his carriage dropped towards the mosaic roof of his tall house, that if human

31

longevity had not been increased they would probably be all right as far as the survival of the race was concerned. With what had once been the normal cycle of life and death, genes might have built up a gradual resistance. It was too late to do anything about it now, though . . .

When the car had landed, Clovis helped Fastina out of it. She smiled, breathing in the rich, heavy air. Africa directly faced the sun and its vegetation was even lusher than it had been. She glanced at Clovis and was about to comment on the view when she thought she caught a peculiar look in his eyes, as if he stared at some secret part of her that she did not know existed—some physical organ of hers which stored the secrets of her unconscious ambitions and her future.

She thought of him for an instant as an ancient, sombre shaman who might cut the organ from her living body and toss it steaming in the still air to make some unholy divination. He smiled at her quietly as he gestured for her to precede him into the gravishute which gaped in the centre of the roof. Perhaps, she thought, he had not been looking into her soul, but his own.

Dropping into the dark hole of the shute, she felt as if she were condemning herself to an irrevocable destiny. Whether her destiny would be good or bad she could not tell.

I'm in a funny state of mind, she thought, as she drifted down. A disordered state of mind, no doubt about that. It must be love . . .

Later they stood drinking aperitifs on the balcony outside the dining room. It looked out over the lake. A great cloud of pink flamingoes flew past, high above the lake. There was a sense of peace now and the silence of the countryside was broken only by the distant call of some wild canine in the forest.

"When we're gone, at least this will remain," said Velusi leaning on the invisible force rail. "When people bothered to debate these abstract issues, some used to think that the human race was a freak—a sport of nature—that we had no business being here at all and no

32

place in the scheme of things. Perhaps they were right."

Fastina smiled. "It doesn't matter now."

"Not to us," Velusi replied, "but there are people about even today who think that the space-dwellers were some sort of mystic agency—you know, like in the old religions—whose purpose was to eliminate human beings, to straighten the biological record, as it were. It matters to them—it's becoming their creed."

"You mean those peculiar people who shave their heads and so on?" Marca asked.

"Yes, poor things." Velusi sighed. "We don't change much, do we? Only a short time ago we had nothing to fear. Our population was small, we had everything we wanted, the world was good—we lived in a paradise, though we didn't know it . . ."

"I knew it," Marca murmured.

"Yes, I suppose you did," Velusi continued. "I remember when you first came to live with us how you would go on and on telling us how perfect our society was compared with the one you'd just left. I could never properly understand why a certain kind of person actually chose to live in the twilight . . ."

"Can you now?" Fastina asked.

"In a way, yes. Those people with their shaven heads are living in a kind of mental twilight already. If you have that mentality, then I suppose you choose to live where it can survive best. That's what I was going to say. In a world without fear the human virtues flourish and become dominant. We've had no violence, no major neuroses for centuries. The space-dwellers somehow managed to put us in our place, made us realise our limitations, made us cultivate the best of what we had. But now fear is back, isn't it? Fear was largely responsible for creating the primitive religions, and fear, of one sort or another, was what fostered the unpleasant elements in even the sophisticated religions. Fear produced repressive societies, totalitarian governments, wars, and the major proportion of sexual perversions, as well, of course, as the multitude of mental perversions—perverse philosophical theories, political systems, religious creed, even artistic expression. Think

33

of the numbers of talented creative people who spent their lives trying to bend their gifts to express some insane notion of the way things should be." Velusi gestured with his glass. "Well, it seems we're back where we started. There's nothing we can do about it—when in the past did a really irrational person ever listen to reason? I'm not a pessimistic man, but I get the feeling that we're going to enter a new dark age which will only end when the last man or woman on Earth dies—and at this rate that could be even sooner than we think . . ."

"You sound like an ancient prophet yourself, Narvo." Marca drained the remainder of his drink. "The apocalypse is at hand, eh?"

CHAPTER THREE

Something to Hide

They ate in Marca's dining room. It was not large. Its walls were decorated with abstract frescoes, vaguely reminiscent of Mayan art. The room was just a little gloomy.

After the meal, Narvo Velusi got up to go. He had guessed the purpose of Fastina's visit.

"I'll see you tomorrow, Clovis," he said. "And I'll tell you then about my own equally unreasonable project." He waved cheerfully and entered the gravishute entrance.

"I wonder what that could be," Marca murmured when he had gone. "I hope it's nothing drastic."

Fastina poured more wine for both of them. "Narvo wouldn't do anything drastic would he? Do you think he's right about what he said? It sounded ominous—and it did seem reasonable."

Marca stretched out in his big chair. "We haven't changed much in all those thousands of years, Fastina. We have the same drives, the same ambitions—presumably the same fears producing the same results. I know that I've felt afraid at times, recently . . ."

"But you've been in space. That's different."

"Not just in space. In fact it's nothing to do with space or any other kind of environment—it's in *me*. I think it always has been."

"Is that what made you go off so suddenly?"

He laughed. "You're still trying to find out about that, aren't you? I promised myself I'd tell no one why I left or what I'm looking for . . ."

"So you're looking for something." She smiled back. "Not someone, by any chance?"

He shook his head. "Not a woman, Fastina, if that's what you're getting at. I don't need to look anyway, when the nicest woman I've ever known is sitting opposite me." He spoke half-jokingly and she looked at him carefully, trying to guess if the statement had been anything more than a pleasant compliment. For an instant he returned her gaze steadily, then looked at the wine. He reached out and refilled their glasses. They were both drinking more than usual.

"It is someone as well," he continued. "Someone with something I want—and even then I'm not sure they have it."

"You're not being fair, Clovis," she said lightly. "You're making it sound more and more intriguing!"

"I'm sorry, Fastina. I suppose there's no harm in mentioning the name of the person. It's Orlando Sharvis . . ."

He glanced at her intently, as if looking for a sign that she recognised the name. It was vaguely familiar, but nothing more.

"No," she said. "It doesn't mean anything. I won't press you any further, Clovis. I'm sorry to have sounded so curious. You're back now, that's the main thing."

He rubbed his lips, nodding abstractedly. "For the time being, anyway," he said quietly.

Now she could not disguise her anxiety. She leant towards him over the table. "You're not leaving again?"

"It might be necessary." He touched her hand. "Don't worry about it, Fastina. My own feelings are as stupid as anyone's. Maybe I'll see sense and forget all about them."

She held his hand tightly and now they looked directly into each other's faces.

"We should enjoy life," she said hesitantly. "Shouldn't we? While we can?"

Still holding her hand, he got up and came round to the couch.

He took her in his arms, pressing her to his body. "Perhaps you're right," he said. His voice was trembling, grim, distant.

36

He kissed her suddenly and she responded, though now she was afraid of him, afraid of something she had released in him. His love-making became urgent, desperate.

They got up together, walking towards the gravishute.

His frantic and tense manner disturbed her, but she knew it was far too late to do anything but let him lead her into the shaft. They rose up together. His grasp on her arm was painful.

They reached the bedroom entrance and he caught the hand-grip, pulling them both to the side of the shaft. They entered his room. It had been darkened and only a little light came through the outer wall.

Surprised, she saw the silhouette of a man against it. A man who held his head in a peculiar way.

In a world without crime, locks and alarms did not exist, so that the man could have entered the room when and how he chose. He was guilty of a crime; an invasion of privacy at very least.

That was not what shocked Marca so much as his recognition of the man. He paused by the gravishute entrance, still gripping Fastina's arm.

"What do you want here, Mr. Take?" he said.

The man did not move, did not speak.

Almost for the first time in his adult life, Clovis Marca allowed anger to get the better of him. He let go of Fastina's arm and plunged across the room towards the dark figure.

"This time I'm getting my explanation," he said, reaching out towards Take.

The intruder moved just before Marca's hands touched him. He moved faster than it should have been possible for an ordinary man to move. He made for the gravishute, but Fastina blocked the entrance with her body. He veered aside and stood stock still again. Then he spoke. His voice was melodious and deep.

"You will never be able to touch me, Clovis Marca. Let me leave here, I mean you no harm, I hope."

"No harm?" Marca was breathing heavily. "You've

been haunting me for months! Who are you? What do you want from me?"

"My name is Take."

"A good name for a thief. What's your real name?"

"I did not come here to steal anything from you. I merely wished to confirm something."

"What?"

"What I guessed you are looking for."

"Be quiet!" Marca glanced anxiously at Fastina.

"You are ashamed?" asked Take.

"No, but it doesn't suit me to reveal what I'm looking for. You can see the sense of that, can't you? Conditions here are no longer normal, I'm not sure you know what it is, anyway."

"I know."

Then Take had leapt to where Fastina stood, pushed her gently aside and jumped into the gravishute, so swiftly that it was impossible to follow his movements.

Clovis ran across the room and followed him into the shute. Above him he heard Take's voice calling a warning.

"You are a fool, Clovis Marca—what you're looking for isn't worth the finding!"

Reaching the roof, Marca saw a small carriage taking off.

His own car was back at the Great Glade. He could call it on his ultrasonic whistle, but it would take too long to get here.

He watched Take's car disappear in the direction of the mountains. He shielded his eyes, trying to see exactly where it was heading, but it was no good.

His face clouded with anger, he walked slowly back over the bright, mosaic roof to the gravishute shaft.

Fastina appeared. Her hair was dishevelled, her expression concerned.

"I couldn't stop him," she said. "I'm sorry."

He took her hand gently, controlling his anger. He shrugged.

"That's all right. He moved too quickly."

"Have you ever seen a man move as fast as that? How does he do it? You know him, don't you?"

"I've seen him, but that was the first time I've spoken to him. I must find out where he comes from. How *could* he know what I'm looking for?"

"If he's staying on daylight Earth, then Central Information could find him for you," she suggested. "But he looked like a twilighter to me—there was something about him . . ."

"I know what you mean. Forget about him. I'll get in touch with Central Information later, as you suggest."

Then he grasped Fastina, pulling her towards him, bending her head back to kiss her, pushing his hands over her body, feeling her arms circle him and her nails dig into his back.

"Oh, Clovis!"

As they lay in bed later he decided to tell her what he was looking for. Since he had made love to her, his original obsession had become more remote and the need for secrecy, at least with her, less important. Also it would be a relief to talk abut it to her.

He began to speak. In the darkness, she listened.

"My father used to talk about Orlando Sharvis," he said, his voice faint and reminiscent. "He was a scientist who lived in the days before the raid. There was never a genius like him, my father said. He had mastered every discipline. Sharvis was not a conventional scientist, not a seeker after knowledge in the ordinary sense, but he had a monumental curiosity. He would experiment for its own sake, just to see what could be made to happen. When the world stopped, he built a laboratory in the twilight region and gathered a group of people about him. They were not all scientists. They decided to build a spaceship to Sharvis's specifications and go to Titan, to set up a colony . . ."

"The Titan expedition—the original one?" She raised herself on her elbow and faced him. "So there was an expedition."

"Yes. Sharvis's experiments, so my father said, had revealed a way of staving off the effects of the space ache for long periods. Sharvis believed that they could stay on Titan long enough to adapt to the conditions there—even

39

if adaptation had to be artificially aided. Sharvis's biological experiments had already got him into trouble in his youth. There had been a war—the Last War we call it now—between the monopolistic commercial companies. Sharvis had been chief of research with one of the companies and had experimented on living prisoners. When the war was over—you remember that it was responsible for the radical change in our society that led to the establishment of our present one . . ."

"I know that much. The commercial organisations destroyed one another. Paseda's party stepped in, nationalised everything and abolished the money system. Go on."

"After it was all over. Sharvis was a wanted criminal, but he managed to go into hiding during the confusion. He would have been caught eventually, I suppose, if it hadn't been for the raid. His experiments, inhuman though they were, had taught him a great deal about human biology. He believed that he could operate surgically to counter the space ache and accelerate adaptation. He made the initial operations on Earth, then they left for Titan."

"So there is a chance that there are people on Titan?"

"I thought so—but there aren't."

"How do you know?"

"I went there in a ship I obtained on Ganymede."

"But surely you couldn't have survived long enough to—?"

"It wasn't pleasant, but I was there long enough to discover that Sharvis's colony had arrived, that it had survived for a while . . . but when I got there all I discovered were skeletons. They were scarcely human skeletons, either. Surgically, Sharvis had changed his Titanians into monsters. I looked for Sharvis himself—or at least a sign of him—but there was nothing. As far as I could tell Sharvis had left Titan."

"But he would be dead by now," she said. "He must have been born at least a hundred years before the raid."

"That's what I was coming to. You see, my father told me that Sharvis was immortal. He said that Sharvis had the power to make others immortal as well."

"And yet you've spent a year looking for him and haven't found a trace. Doesn't that prove that your father was wrong?"

"There *have* been rumours. I believe that Alodios discovered where Sharvis was."

"Alodios!"

Alodios, the great artist, had disappeared at about the same time as Marca. His disappearance had been even more inexplicable than Marca's.

"Yes. I came back to see if I could pick up the trail again—find out where Alodios went."

"What about Take?"

"I know nothing of Take—unless he is Sharvis's agent."

"But you still haven't told me what you want Sharvis for. Do you think he might have a means of reviving our fertility—or creating artificial sperm in some way?"

"He might have. But my reason for finding him is rather more selfish."

She kissed his shoulder softly, moving her left hand over his chest.

"I can't believe you're selfish, Clovis."

"Can't you?"

Once again she felt that disturbing, desperate grip on her body as he caressed her.

"I'll tell you what I want from Sharvis," he began grimly, but she put her mouth to his and kissed him.

She no longer wanted to know what he was looking for. She was afraid for herself and for him.

"Don't tell me," she murmured. "Just love me, Clovis. Love me."

CHAPTER FOUR

Something to Forget

As they were preparing to get up some hours later, the laser-screen in the corner signalled. Marca wondered who it was and whether to ignore it. He decided to answer it since he had anyway meant to get up earlier. He went to a cupboard and took a yellow cloak from it, wrapping it round him.

He activated the screen.

Andros Almer's face appeared. He could see into the darkened room and his expression changed as he saw Fastina lying in the bed.

"So you weren't unlucky, after all," he said to her.

She smiled regretfully. "Sorry, Andros."

Marca looked perplexed. "What do you want, Andros?"

"I've just had news that a ship is heading for the Sector Eight landing field," Almer said, still looking at Fastina. "Due to get here soon."

"What of it?"

"Well, as far as we can tell, the ship's coming from Titan. We think it's the Titan expedition returning."

"Impossible."

"Maybe. I'm going to meet it, anyway. Something could have activated the automatic return system. I thought you might like to see it, too, Clovis. I screened Brand Calax, but he's busy, he says, with the plans for his own expedition. My guess is that he just doesn't want to see proof of the truth. Fastina might like to come, too. After all . . ."

"Thanks, Andros, we'll probably see you at the field."

Marca switched off. "Your husband could be on it," he said. "Do you think you want to see him?"

"I'll come," she said, swinging her legs to the floor.

The ship came silently down. It landed on the deserted field under the blazing, motionless sun. It was a big, complex ship of a golden plastic alloy that was turned to deep red by the sunlight. It landed with a faint whisper of sound like a murmur of apology, as if aware that its presence was unwelcome.

Three figures started forward over the yielding surface of the spacefield. In the distance, to their right, were the partially abandoned hangars and control rooms: slim buildings in pale yellow and blue.

The voice in Marca's earbead said: "Shall we open up?"

"You might as well," he said.

As they reached the spherical ship, the lock began to open, twenty feet above them.

They paused, listening for a familiar sound they did not want to hear.

There was no sound.

Drifting up on their gravstraps, they paused at the open airlock. Marca looked at Fastina. "Andros and I will go in first—we've seen this sort of thing before. You haven't . . ."

"I'll go in with you."

The smell from the airlock was nauseating. It was a combination of foul air and rotting tissue.

Andros Almer pursed his lips. "Let's go, then." He lead the way through the airlock into a short metal tunnel.

The first body was there.

It was a woman's body. It was naked, contorted and it stank. The grey flesh was filthy, the hair was matted, the upturned face was twisted, with wide eyes and lips snarling back from the teeth; the cheeks were hollow. The flesh showed signs of laceration and her fingernails seemed imbedded in her right breast.

"Ierna Colo," Almer murmured. "Pyens Colo's daughter. I told the old fool to make her stay behind."

Fastina turned away. "I didn't realise . . ."

"You'd better wait outside," Marca said.

"No."

In the main control cabin they found two others. A man's body lay over a woman's. For some reason the man's body had corrupted much faster while the woman's was still almost whole. She seemed to be embracing him, the rictus of her mouth giving her the appearance of revelling in obscene joy—though it was really plain that she had been trying to ward the man off.

"Hamel Berina," Almer said. It was Fastina's husband.

"The woman's Jara Ferez, isn't it?" Fastina asked weakly. "Jara Ferez?"

"Yes," Marca replied. Jara had always liked Hamel. That was probably the reason why she had volunteered for the expedition.

The remains of the rest of the crew were also there. Some of the bones had been gnawed, some split. A skull had been broken open.

Face taut, Andros operated the door to the galley. He glanced inside.

"Enough supplies for at least another six months," he said. "We made the controls simple enough, in case things got really bad. All they had to do was break the seals on the packs."

"But they didn't, did they?" Fastina said, her voice breaking.

"You'd think they'd retain some survival instincts," Marca murmured.

"Isn't that a definition of madness, Clovis?" Andros cleared his throat. "Something that makes you act against your natural instincts? Look—that's how we lost contact."

He pointed at the smashed cameras above. Their protective cases had been torn open. Everything breakable had been destroyed. Machinery was twisted, papers torn, streamers of microtape programmes were scattered everywhere.

Andros shook his head. "All those tests we made on them, all that time spent training them, conditioning them—all the precautions we took . . ." He sighed.

Marca picked up a torn length of microtape and began twisting it round his finger.

"They were intelligent people," Andros went on. "They knew what to expect and how to fight it. They had courage, initiative, common sense and self-control—yet in six months they became insane, bestial travesties of human beings. Look at them—grotesque animals, more debased than we could guess . . ."

He glanced at a wall. He pointed at the pictures drawn on it in what seemed to be dried human blood. "That sort of thing was done quite early on, I should think." He kicked at a pile of filthy rags. "Titan! We can't survive in space for a matter of months, let alone centuries. These people were sacrificed for nothing."

Marca sighed. "We could revive the woman—Jara —for about ten minutes. She's not too far gone."

Andros rubbed his face. "Is it worth it, Clovis?"

"No." Marca's voice was hollow. "It's unlikely they were able to get at the recorders. They should tell us what happened."

"We don't really need to check, do we?" Almer said.

Marca shook his head slowly. He put his arm round Fastina's shoulders. "Let's get out of this ship."

As they left the airlock and drifted towards the spaceport buildings the voice in Marca's earbead said: "Any instructions?"

"Destroy it," Marca said. "And don't release the news. Morale's bad enough as it is."

They climbed into Almer's car on the edge of the field.

The ship had an automatic destruction mechanism that could only be operated from base. All ships had the same device in the event of space ache getting out of hand as it had done on the Titan vessel.

Behind them the golden ship crumpled. There was a brilliant flash and they heard the sharp, smacking sound as it was vaporised.

Fastina's face was pale.

"Do you think Calax will change his mind now?" Marca asked Almer.

Almer sneered. "Calax? Not after we've destroyed the

evidence. Mark my words, he just won't believe us."

"You think we should have kept the ship to show him?"

"I doubt if he'd have let us show it to him," Almer said. "Calax doesn't obey any rational instincts as far as I know."

"You seem to have some personal grudge against Calax," Marca said. "It's almost as if you hate him."

"I hate everyone," Andros said savagely. "I hate the whole horrible mess."

Marca stretched back on his couch, trying to get the images in the ship out of his mind. He could see them all, still, twisted faces, contorted bodies, filth, wreckage, bones.

Memento mori the world could do without, he thought. That was why he had told them to destroy the ship. If they ran away from a dying man at a party, what would that sight do to them?

Fastina was sitting upright, staring over the countryside as they moved along. Marca knew it would be stupid to try to comfort her at this stage. She was in a state of shock.

"What do you want to do now?" Almer was asking him. "Can I take you both back to your house, Clovis?" His voice sounded ragged.

"No thanks, Andros. Take us to the Great Glade, my car's there."

The air carriage wheeled in the cloudless sky as Almer accelerated and headed for the south western flower forest.

CHAPTER FIVE

Something Ominous

Four days later, Clovis Marca left Fastina at his house and went to see Tarn Yoluf of Central Information.

Fastina had recovered from her shock but was still occasionally pensive. She had been unable completely to rid her mind of the sight of her dead husband in the spaceship and at length Marca had decided to leave her alone for a while so that she could, as she had suggested, sleep for a couple of days and hope that that would be enough to clear her head of the images in the ship and the guilt that she felt when she remembered them.

The horror he had witnessed had, for the moment at least, convinced Clovis Marca of the futility of his own search for the legendary Orlando Sharvis. Doubtless Sharvis had died on Titan, too.

Situated on the edge of a flower forest, the Central Information building stood two storeys above ground and fifty storeys below. Tarn Yoluf's big, computer-lined office looked out over the sunlit forest and a smooth intervening lawn.

Yoluf sat at his desk surrounded by laser-screens and control consoles. He was a tall, slim man in middle age. He had very fair hair and a pale, anaemic face. His eyes were pale blue and in contrast to the rest of his features his very full red lips looked as if they had been painted. He was wearing a high-collared lilac shirt and green tights.

Marca told him that he wanted to know the whereabouts of Take. Yoluf started at once. He punched buttons

47

and operated controls but after an hour his records had come up with nothing.

"I'll try my sections, Clovis," he said. His voice was extremely high-pitched. "But not all of them are operating these days."

Later he sat back in his chair and spread his long hands in apology.

"No trace yet, Clovis."

Marca shrugged. The problem of Take had become less important since he had made his decision. "I'm sorry to have troubled you, Tarn. The man's made me uncomfortable, that's all. As I said, he seems to have been following me for some time. The other day I discovered him in my house . . ."

"Surely not?" Yoluf looked shocked. "Uninvited?"

"Yes. I thought if I could find him and warn him not to do anything like it again, it would be sufficient to make him leave me in peace. For all I know he's vanished for good, anyway."

"You mentioned that his reflexes were abnormally fast. Your description of him could hardly fit anyone—but we're stumped, Clovis. He sounds like a twilight man, but we've records of all surviving twilight people and he's not amongst them. Twilighters are about the only people who'd invade a man's house like that . . ."

Marca nodded. "Thanks, anyway, Tarn."

Yoluf chewed his lower lip. "Hang on for a moment, Clovis. There's still a chance . . ."

"It's not really important . . ."

"I'd rather make sure we've checked everywhere." He turned to one of his consoles and began pressing more buttons. "You know what we need? A passport system like the old days. To hell with the freedom of the individual. How am I supposed to run an information centre without a decent system?"

Marca smiled and sat down in the chair opposite Yoluf. "You're a frustrated bureaucrat."

"We wouldn't be where we are today without the bureaucrats, Clovis." Yoluf jokingly wagged his finger. "It was the civil servants who helped turn over the State from

48

its old restrictive form into the present one. Don't underestimate the bureaucratic mentality. You might think that the administration's decision to wind itself up was a good idea—I don't."

"It simply happened that way," Marca said good humouredly. "Since we only had a short time to go we suggested that anyone who wished to give up their work could do so. Many are still continuing. You are, for one."

"It's not the same, Clovis. Where's yesterday's smooth-running administrative machine? Bits! Bits without links or a properly working motor. If the machine were running right do you think it would take this long to find your mysterious friend?"

"I suppose not," Marca admitted as Yoluf fussed with his controls. "You think some sort of emergency government should be formed?"

"I don't make decisions of that order. That's up to you. But anyone can see that our civilisation's crumbling to pieces day by day. We need a firmer government—not none at all!"

"Firmer government? You're really beginning to sound like someone from pre-raid days. What good do firmer governments ever do that isn't overbalanced by the problems they cause?"

"You used the word 'emergency' yourself, Clovis. Isn't this one? Ah, here's Mars . . ."

A light was blinking above one of the laser-screens and a face appeared on it. The colours were in bad register and the man's face was a dirty green.

Yoluf pointed at the screen. "There's another example of what's happening. See that colour? We can't get a mechanic to fix it. At this rate there'll be complete chaos in a matter of months. Didn't they always say that when communications began to break down that was a sign of the beginning of the end? We'll all be dead sooner than we think . . ." The signal buzzed and Yoluf flicked a switch. "Yes?"

The man on the screen was already talking. ". . . no information regarding the man you call Mr. Take. No ship registered to him. No one of his description or name has landed in a passenger ship. We haven't checked everywhere. Some of the old mine pits are deep enough to hide a small ship . . ."

Yoluf's tone was exasperated. "Then keep trying." He broke contact well before his message could get to Mars. He shook his head. "I used to be all but omniscient a year ago—as far as people's public lives were concerned. Now all I get are mysteries! We were asked about your whereabouts and lost you half the time. We're still being asked about Alodios and we can't find *him*. Now this man Take can't be traced. You're looking at a broken man, Clovis! Somebody who's gone from omniscience to impotence in less than twelve months. I'm going insane!"

"Aren't we all?" smiled Marca. "What did happen to Alodios?"

"I told you, we don't know. We found his air carriage without any trouble. It was in the twilight region. Sector 119."

"I know the area—near the sea, isn't it?"

"Yes. South American continent."

"Do you think he killed himself?" Marca was now almost certain that this was what had happened to the great artist. There had been one or two other suicides, especially among artists.

"That's what I do think," Yoluf said emphatically, "but not everyone will have it. I have to keep trying—with the best means at my disposal, which isn't saying a great deal these days . . ."

"Ah, well," said Marca as he got up to leave, "struggle on as best you can, Tarn."

Yoluf shrugged. "What's the point?"

"None, I suppose. If you do hear anything of Take you'll let me know, will you?"

"If I can get in touch with you," said Yoluf bitterly, turning his attention back to his instruments.

On his way to visit Narvo Velusi, Marca saw smoke rising in the distance. He was crossing a great, grassy plain that covered the region once known as northern France. The breeze whispered through the grass and around the air

50

car and a few white clouds moved slowly through the deep blue sky. As always, the sun hung motionless above him. In this area it was in a position of mid-afternoon.

It was definitely thick, black smoke he could see ahead. It was very unusual to see smoke at all. Curious, he guided the car towards it.

Later he saw that it was a building; an ordinary mobile house. Strictly speaking the house was not burning, but its contents were. Marca took the car down to see if there was anyone in trouble.

On the far side of the building, obscured at first by the billowing smoke, he saw a small group of figures standing watching the blaze. There were about eight people there, all dressed in black robes like ancient monks' habits, their heads shaven and their faces covered in masks of the same black material.

There was little doubt, Marca decided, that the fire had been started deliberately.

As he circled closer the bald skulls went back and masked faces peered at him. He felt bound to shout to them.

"Anything wrong? Can I help?"

One of them called back: "You can help cleanse the universe of evil by joining us, brother."

Marca was astonished. The word 'evil' was an archaic term rarely heard these days.

"What are you doing?" he called.

"We are ridding the world of the artifacts of mankind." answered another tonelessly.

"Who are you?" Marca could hardly believe that these people were from daylight Earth. Twilight Earth had had, at one time, its share of peculiar cults, but that was normal and even the cults had died out in later years as the twilight folk became more and more introverted.

"We are the guilty!" a new voice screamed up at him.

With a shudder, Marca took the car into a rapid climb and fled away.

He looked back once at the smoke. It seemed to him that it came from the first signal fire that heralded the apocalypse he had joked about a few days earlier.

He knew that, unless it was checked, it would soon be one of many fires. His own upbringing in the twilight region had made him familiar with the darker side of human nature, but he had never expected to see anything like it in the daylight world.

How could this cult's activities be checked? There was no method known to his society: there had been no violence there for centuries. To take the reactionary step, as Yoluf had half-jokingly suggested, of forming a 'firmer' government was unthinkable to people trained to respect the freedom of the individual at all costs. Yet here was a situation that could only be fought by a society of the old sort.

There was no doubt about it, he thought, as he passed over the forests of the Rhine and neared Narvo Velusi's house. Narvo had been right: Fear created fear and violence created violence.

It was with a feeling of despair that he landed on the roof of his old friend's house.

No one more than himself had appreciated the social and natural paradise of daylight Earth; no one had valued it more or realised how ideal it had been.

Now, it seemed, the world he had loved was not even to die gracefully.

Fear was back, and with it the old terrors, the old mental aberrations, the old superstitions, the old religions. He knew the pattern. He had studied it in the text books. He knew how little power rational argument had when faced with minds turned sick by fear. He knew how quickly a cult of the kind he had seen could proliferate and dominate a society and then split internally and become several warring sects. And his society, without means of aiding the cult was probably the most vulnerable in history.

His paradise threatened to become a hell and there was little he could think of doing that would stop the process now that it had begun.

CHAPTER SIX

Something to Hope For

"They call themselves the Brotherhood of Guilt," Narvo Velusi said, pouring Marca a drink. "Originally they simply decided to give up sexual relations because it was pointless—though it hadn't stopped anyone in the past. Well, you can guess what followed that decision, can't you? The masks and the rest were explained by them as being necessary so that a person's sex could not be distinguished. Up to now they have been harmless, in that they haven't actually done anything violent. This burning you mention must be the first—we'd have heard of others. I suspect that the house belongs to one of their number. It's an odd syndrome, Marca, but one we could have anticipated if we had not been so obsessed with the idea of our ultimate fate."

"What do you mean?" Marca noticed his hand was trembling as he took the drink and walked towards the window to look out over the forest of dark pines that lay below the hill on which Narvo Velusi had sited his house.

"Well, while denying nature in themselves, they say that what is not 'natural' is 'evil'—you're quite right, that is the word you heard them use—and that therefore all human artifacts are evil."

Marca shook his head. "It doesn't make sense, Narvo." He took a sip of his drink. "I know these peculiar ideas never do, but it's not that I really meant. I can't understand how a well-adjusted society could go rotten in such a brief time. Even in the past things didn't happen so rapidly."

53

Narvo joined him at the window. "You're quite right—but in the past they had various means of resisting and controlling such outbreaks. They were a recurring cancer in the body of society, but usually they were promptly cauterised from the main body—segregated in some way. Sometimes they were not cut out in time—so you got the fanatical Christianity of what the Christian society later called their 'middle ages'—and the equally fanatical black magic cults and secret societies. A few hundred years later, when non-religious leaders were dominating the world, you got the madness of naziism; still later there was the meritocratic system which virtually controlled the whole world at one stage. And every time, of course, human society managed, through violence and struggle, to rectify and destroy the cancer. But now, Clovis, there will not be time to do any such thing . . ."

"Are you sure?" Marca's tone was bleak.

"The only thing that would save us," Narvo smiled ironically, "is salvation itself. If our poisoned cells could be revived. It is a pattern, you see. There's always a pattern."

"Isn't there something positive we can do, Narvo? Isn't there some goal we could give people—even . . . ?" He broke off and stared at his friend miserably.

"Even if it means lying to them?" Velusi said gently. "Perhaps there is, but you can see what's happening, can't you? A lie or two might halt the process for a little while, but it wouldn't stop it for long enough. And how would lying affect us, Clovis? There's no doubt in my mind that we should find ourselves corrupted, needing to gather more and more personal power in order to control the means of communication, keep the truth from the majority. It has started, you see. Even we are affected by what is happening. We can't fail to be."

Marca threw down his glass. It bounced across the sunlit room and struck a wall. "Can't we divert them? Can't we appeal to their better instincts? All these people were sane, rational human beings up to a few months ago. Their ethical instincts have only been buried. If we can revive them . . ."

"An ethic is simply a system of survival," Velusi said. "What does an ethic mean when there is no chance of survival?"

Marca put his hands to his face, shaking his head mutely.

Velusi went over and picked up the glass. It was unbroken. He filled it and took it back to Marca.

"Clovis," he said after a while, "I mentioned the other day that I had a scheme—a scheme as irrational as Brand Calax's, but one that might work to some extent."

"What is it?"

"It's a stupid plan. It seems ludicrous even to me when I think about it. It is just something I thought of. I want to build a big transmitter—a bigger radio transmitter than any that has ever existed. And then I want to send a message on it."

"A message? Why? What message?" Marca tried to clear his head and give his attention to the old man.

"Just a message that will travel through space—that will go to the other intelligent races in other star systems and galaxies. We know they exist—the space-dwellers told us that much. It will be a message that will survive long after we have perished. It'll be a kind of monument—it'll just say that we once lived. They probably won't even be able to understand the message . . ."

"What will it say?"

Velusi went over to a deep, high-backed chair and sat down.

"Just 'We are here'," he said.

"Just that?" Marca shrugged. "But we won't be . . ."

"I know, but someone might follow the message back—the transmitter will continue to work after we are dead, you see. Another race might find us, discover our records, and we'll live on in a way—in their minds and their books. Do you see, Clovis?" Velusi looked up eagerly at him.

Clovis nodded. "I do, Narvo, but is there any point? I mean, could you convince the others that the transmitter would be worth building?"

"I'm going to try at the Great Glade tomorrow. The

message could be picked up by all manner of creatures, you see. Perhaps some of them will be like us. The message will convey our pride in our existence, our gratitude to the biological accident that gave us the ability to reason." Velusi sighed, looking up at Marca. "I know it's pathetic, Clovis, but it's the best thing I could think of."

"It's better than anything I can think of," Marca said, putting his hand on the old man's shoulder. He saw that Narvo Velusi was crying. "I'll come with you to the glade tomorrow. I'll back you up. Work on the transmitter will employ hundreds of people. It will be therapeutic at very least, eh?" He made an effort and smiled at his friend.

"It will be a kind of immortality," Velusi said, weeping openly now. "Won't it, Clovis?"

"Yes," Marca said in pity, "a kind of immortality."

CHAPTER SEVEN

Somewhere to Go

Fastina sat in bed eating the meal Marca had brought her. "So Narvo convinced them?" she said with her mouth full.

"Many of them. Obviously I don't know as much about human nature as I thought. They're wondering where to site the transmitter and everything." He sat down beside her on the bed. "How do you feel?"

She grinned at him. "Fine. How are yoou? Have you given up the search for Sharvis?"

"There doesn't seem any point in going on with it."

She put down her fork and took his hand. "I'm glad, Clovis. We've got the best part of two centuries together. We should be grateful."

He smiled. "Do you think we can stay together that long?"

"The first hundred years are the worst," she laughed. "Anyway, you're a very mysterious person and I'm sure it will take that long to get to know you. I'm not as simple as I look, either." She gave him the tray. "I'd like to get up and go out now. Where shall we go?"

"Anywhere," he said. "Anywhere you like."

Lying side by side, naked under the hot sun, they let the air car drift out above the sea. Virtually tideless now, the South Atlantic went sparkling to the edge of the world.

They talked idly, holding hands. He spoke of his childhood and his morbid, melancholy father; of his mother, who had also been his sister. He spoke without rancour or embarrassment, for the times were now distant and unreal.

The twilight world had become the same strange place to him as it had always been to her. He told her how Velusi had had his house in Kashmir the year he had walked towards the sun. He had arrived there, almost dead with fatigue and starvation.

Velusi and his wife had liked him. Velusi had probably been a little amused by him, too. They had adopted him and Velusi had begun to teach him all that the old man knew himself; though Clovis had already known a great deal from his own reading in his father's tower. Velusi was then Deputy Chairman of the Council and had been able to instruct Clovis Marca in the ideas and methods of the politics of the daylight region. He had encouraged him to go into public life when the time came.

"I wanted to, anyway. I admired this world so much, you see."

The carriage drifted on. They raised the canopy and made love. They ate and drank. Later, they settled the car on the water so that it rocked on the gentle waves. They swam in the warm ocean, splashing and laughing in the salt sea, making it foam around the hull of the carriage.

Time passed and they did not care. They became filled with a euphoric happiness and a pleasure in each other's company that could only be felt away from society. They both experienced a love that they knew to be elemental and probably never to be repeated. They wanted it to last. They had brought no means of telling the time and they had all they needed to eat. They sailed on across the calm Atlantic, hardly even talking now, but smiling a great deal and laughing sometimes, too, and staying very close together as if they feared that once they parted they would not find each other again.

There were no strong winds on the ocean, no cold nights, no wild tides. The sea was at peace and so were they. They saw a whale. It was a huge adult blue whale, nearly a hundred and twenty feet long, the largest beast that had ever lived. It was moving over the surface at speed, sometimes lifting its great bulk clean out of the water. They followed it. It swam along gently for a while and then dived deep into the ocean. They saw a school of fifty or so dolphins not long after, chasing one another through the sea.

Still later, they saw seabirds wheeling in flocks in the distance.

The sun was far behind them now, not far from the horizon, and it was a little cooler but still pleasant.

The carriage was swept by a sudden current towards an island. It was thickly wooded and a yellow beach ran down to the sea. The sky behind the island was orange and darkening and they knew that this was almost the twilight region; but the island was pleasant and they ran about in the sand, picking up seashells and pieces of coral. They went to sleep on the beach, with their toes pointing towards the sea.

When they woke up, it seemed colder, and an animal was screaming from behind them in the jungle. They laughed, but ran down to the air carriage and wrapped themselves in cloaks.

Then he took the carriage into the sky and headed swiftly towards the sun.

They landed on the ocean again when they were back, and swam and made love again, but their earlier pleasure was gone and soon they went home into Africa and his house beside Lake Tanganyika.

Even here they ignored the laser-screen when it signalled and spent a great deal of their time together in bed, or walking along the shore of the lake arm in arm.

One day Fastina sighed. "If only we could have children," she said, dabbling her bare foot in the lake and looking out over the tree-covered hills that were framed against the hot sky. "Look what there is for them to enjoy."

Marca decided to go to Narvo Velusi's house and see how the work on his transmitter was going.

A month had passed.

He headed towards Europe in the air carriage shaped like a golden bird in flight. The time, he thought, meant nothing to Fastina, with her barren womb.

It seemed, however, that they were bound together now,

perhaps until death. How the link had been forged, he did not understand, but it *had* been forged and neither would ever be able to stay away from the other for long. There might never be pleasure again, only pain, but that would not matter.

He could not explain his knowledge: Love, as he understood it, was not what they had, but love was there in all its forms. Hate was there, too, now, and anger and a melancholy bitterness, and a need for her body that was not any sort of love or hate, but a blind hunger that terrified him. He could understand how such unbearable emotion could drive lovers to suicide.

It was unbearable now. That was why he needed to go away from her and yet seek other company than his own.

The automatic force screen leapt around the carriage as he pushed it to its maximum speed.

The tension had begun to leave him as he saw the Rhineland ahead and reached Velusi's house.

CHAPTER EIGHT

Something to Fight

The huge apparatus took the form of a gigantic sculpture in blue steel and gold wire. It overlooked the Black Sea, rising hundreds of feet high, each piece shining and vibrating slightly in the breeze. It was still surrounded by its tall scaffolding. Its central sections at base were almost half a mile in diameter; between them ran delicate webs, threads of copper, coils of silver, triangles and squares of shimmering greens and reds.

On a high platform above the apparatus stood two figures, dwarfed by the great structure.

"There's still a lot to do," Narvo Velusi said to Clovis Marca. "We haven't begun to install the power yet."

Marca folded his arms and looked down at the transmitter. He knew that it could have been built in a more compact form and cased in some kind of cabinet, but he understood why Velusi had chosen to build it this way. It was not only visible to all those involved in working on it, it was also extremely beautiful, somehow complementing the simplicity of the message they intended to send.

"It's very impressive, Narvo," he said.

"Thank you. It really does seem to have cheered a lot of people up." He smiled. "The work's going faster than I anticipated. We might have to invent a few technical hitches."

A black air carriage began to circle down towards them. It came level with the platform. In it stood a man wearing a loose, flowing black cloak that enclosed his whole body. Attached to the cloak was a hood of the same material.

The hood hid the man's face in shadow.

"May I join you?"

Marca recognised the voice as Andros Almer's.

"Hello, Andros," he said, as the man stepped from the car and on to the platform.

Andros nodded to them and pushed his hood back slightly to peer down at the transmitter. Far below tiny figures could be seen at work.

Marca saw that he was wearing a dark blue mask over the top half of his pale face. The mask was edged in scarlet and like the hooded cloak was of heavy, rich material. On Almer's hands there were matching gloves in dark blue, worked with scarlet, and on his feet were soft, red, knee-length boots.

" 'We are here', eh?" Almer's voice was dry. "Perhaps 'We were here' would be a better message, Narvo?"

Velusi looked uncomfortably at Marca. "Andros thinks there are better uses for the transmitter, Clovis."

Almer turned with a swirl of his heavy cloak, raising one gloved hand. "I have no intention of interfering, Narvo. It is your project. It simply seemed a good idea to broadcast rather more information, to give whoever heard it a better idea of who we were and where to find us."

"That would defeat the whole spirit of the idea, surely?" Clovis frowned. "Can't you see that, Andros?"

"It simply seems a waste, that's all, Clovis." Almer's voice was acid now. "To build this great contrivance and make so little use of it." Almer shrugged. "I wonder what other projects of this kind we'll see in the near future?"

"What do you mean?" Velusi asked, pushing his old hand through his hair. Marca noticed that it was beginning to grey. "Other projects?"

"I'd admit that this one isn't as hopeless as Calax's Titan ship—at least it has a definite, understandable purpose . . ."

"The Titan ship has a purpose," Marca interrupted, "if only to occupy Calax's mind. How's the building going?"

"Oh, rapidly, rapidly. Yes, soon Calax will be off for Titan and that's the last we shall see of him—unless he returns in the manner of the first expedition." Almer moved arrogantly towards his air car. "Well, give my regards to Fastina, Clovis. I must get back to my own affairs. My men are waiting . . ."

"Your *what*?" Marca was incredulous. He had only heard a phrase like that in an historical drama.

Andros ignored him, stepped into his car and swept away.

"What did he say, Narvo?" he asked.

"His men." Narvo repeated quietly, looking down at the transmitter to avoid Marca's eyes.

"*His!*" The concept of other people 'belonging' to a particular person was even more archaic than the term 'evil' which he had heard a month earlier. "Was he joking, Narvo? What's he doing?"

Velusi's tone was over-controlled when he replied. "The Brotherhood of Guilt fired several more houses while you were away. They didn't actually burn the houses, of course, because they won't catch fire, but they destroyed everything that could be burned inside them. And the last two houses they set fire to didn't belong to their own members—a woman was badly burned trying to put the blaze out in her house. Some people, particularly Andros, didn't see why the Brotherhood should be allowed to go about destroying at will while everyone looked on passively . . ."

"So they formed themselves into a group against the Brotherhood, is that it?"

Velusi nodded. "I think *vigilante* is the term they found from somewhere. Andros became their leader—he seemed to like the idea, Clovis."

"I see you were right," Marca sighed. "It was bound to happen, as you said. But I find it hard to believe a man of Andros's training and intelligence would give himself over to such an idea . . ."

"He argues on an old theme, Clovis. Desperate times, he says, require desperate measures."

"So now there are two sources of that cancer you mentioned," Marca murmured, "and if the pattern stays true, there will be more."

"Well, the way it was in the past was that the cancers

helped destroy one another, but, as I told you, I doubt if there will be time left for that now." Velusi touched his gravstrap. "Come, let's get back to the ground. You've seen the transmitter. What about coming to my house for a meal?"

As they sank down gently, Marca said: "I think I'd like to have a look at Brand's spaceship, if you don't mind, Narvo."

"Very well. It's only a couple of hundred miles from here."

They were using Fastina's air car and when Velusi had walked around talking to some of the people working on the transmitter, they got into it and headed for the mountains of Turkey where Calax's Titan ship was under construction.

As they rode towards Turkey, Velusi said: "It's not a question of knowledge and reason, you see. Clovis—it's essentially a question of temperament and strength of mind. Andros had given up. Brand, in his way, has given up, too. In the past we were always ruled by our unconscious drives—even when we knew they were there—reason simply tempered instinct. Andros knows what's happening to him, but he doesn't seem to care any more. I think it's because of Fastina . . ."

"She told me that he was attracted to her, but I didn't think it was a very strong attraction."

"Deep enough, perhaps. Ah, we're nearing the mountains."

In a wide valley, the heavy outlines of Calax's ship could be seen as they descended. The sharp peaks of the mountains, formed into their present shape by the upheavals that had come with the raid, surrounded the valley. The spaceship hull was complete and men were currently fitting its machinery.

They found Brand Calax inside the ship directing the positioning of the compact drive unit. Marca was surprised to see how gaunt and grim-faced he had become. He greeted them civilly enough. "Hello Narvo—Clovis. It's coming along. When we're finished she'll be the best ship ever built. I've got complete simulated Earth environment which will help stave off the space ache. She's about the fastest thing there is, which will help get me there and back quicker and allow me to spend more time on Titan. If there's—" they all stood aside to let the mechanics through as they carried various pieces of equipment into the drive chamber—"if there's anyone on Titan, I'll find 'em."

Marca could have told Brand Calax the truth about Titan, but he had decided that it would not be fair to spoil the man's dream. Even if he died, Calax had that right to die in the manner he chose.

Calax peered into the drive chamber, checking something against the plans he held in his hand. He straightened up, leaning on his other hand against the cold, dark metal of the bulkhead. Later, the interior would be coated with several layers of other materials, and the shell itself was in fact three divided layers with force fields between them.

"People have been really kind," Calax said. "I've had more than I need volunteering to help put the ship together. I'm going to call her *The Orlando Sharvis,* after the man who commanded the colonising expedition . . ."

Though startled to hear the name, Marca said calmly: "Sharvis wasn't a particularly heroic figure, by all accounts. Didn't he do biological experiments on living human beings, things like that?"

"Maybe he had to," Calax said. "Besides, it depends how you look at it. Sharvis had vision and guts. I don't care about the rest of his character, good or bad."

Marca walked around the ship. It was relatively cold in there and he shivered slightly as he went to the entrance and peered out. The airlock had not been installed as yet. He blinked in the strong sunlight, reached into a pocket and brushed darkened lenses over his eyes.

In the foothills of the mountains he thought he saw some people standing motionless, watching the ship.

"Who are those men over there?" he called to Calax.

Brand Calax joined him. "They're from that damned Brotherhood of Guilt cult. They've been there for days.

They don't do anything but stare at us, but I'm afraid they may try some sort of attack. From what I've heard they've already done damage. I'll say that for Andros Almer, he was wise to act swiftly and protect us against them."

"Have they shown any sign that they would attack?" Velusi asked from behind him.

"No, but you know what they think of machinery and the like. A ship like this would be a prime target for them I shouldn't wonder."

"You're probably right." Marca touched his gravstrap and drifted down to the ground. The other two followed him.

"Miona Pelva and Quiro Beni have joined them, I heard," said Velusi, referring to two ex-councillors they had known.

"Incredible!" said Calax. "Decent, intelligent people."

The masked, bald, heavily-robed men and women stared in their direction. Whereas earlier they had worn clothes of any dark material, now they all wore brown.

"Some of them flog one another, by all accounts," Calax said as he led them towards a temporary building where he had his living quarters. "It's part of the punishment for their guilt apparently. I may be stupid, but I can't see what they feel to be guilty about. Still, so long as they don't interfere with me, they can stand there for the next two hundred years for all I care."

"You think they might start something?" Marca asked as they reached the single-storey building and went inside. The room they entered was functional and undecorated. They sat on hard chairs while Calax operated the food dispenser in one corner.

"They might," Calax nodded, "but they've no weapons as yet, only fire. If they want weapons, of course, they'll have to manufacture them in some way and luckily Andros is keeping a firm check on the stores of supplies they'd need. I think we'll be all right."

Marca turned to Velusi. "What authority has Andros to do all this? Has anything been voted on at all?"

"More or less," Velusi said. "A lot of people agreed to

give him temporary powers to deal with the emergency."

"I see." Marca accepted the plate Calax put before him.

"There's only one way of countering this that I can see," Velusi told Marca as they ate. "And that's for you to reform the official council before it's too late."

"How many of us are there left?" Marca asked cynically. "If some of them have joined the Brotherhood and Andros is going it alone, there can't be many."

"We can hold a new election or co-opt fresh members," Velusi suggested.

Marca nodded reluctantly. He did not like to admit to his old friend that his heart was no longer in politics, that, in spite of the threat of the Brotherhood and Andros Almer's vigilantes, he was too obsessed with his personal affairs to consider seriously becoming chairman of the Council again.

"You are still the most respected man in public life, Clovis," Velusi told him. "The majority of the people would follow your leadership willingly. It would give us the chance to put a stop to Almer's ambitions before he gained too much power."

"Are you sure the people would be behind me, Narvo?" he asked. "And would there be time to stop Almer?"

"You could find out!" Brand Calax had been listening. He leaned across his plate, gesticulating with his spoon. "Narvo's thinking straight at last. My feeling is that someone like Almer's needed to deal with the Brotherhood, but we could find ourselves needing someone to deal with Almer in time. Let's act now."

"It would mean restricting people's liberty . . ." Marca shook his head, perplexed. "I couldn't do it. My conscience . . ."

"We've got to make the best of a bad situation, Marca," Velusi reminded him. "Now Almer's evidently got an appetite for power he'll want more. It's obvious."

"I'd have to think more seriously about it," Marca said. He was playing for time, he knew. He just did not want the responsibility any longer.

"You'd better make up your mind soon, Clovis," Calax

warned him. "When I come back from Titan with my good news I want to find a few people still alive to hear it."

They left a short time later. The little group of Brotherhood members were still standing there, watching them impassively.

Brand Calax returned to his ship, *The Orlando Sharvis.*

BOOK TWO

CHAPTER ONE

Men of Action

Marca soon discovered that he could not stay away from Fastina for long and he decided to return home after only three days at Narvo Velusi's house. A further incentive to leave was offered by Velusi's somewhat accusing eye; the old man was plainly waiting impatiently for Marca to make his decision.

He left for Lake Tanganyika.

"I'll decide what to do once I'm there," he told Velusi.

The golden air car took him home and he found Fastina asleep.

Resisting an urge to wake her, he wandered around the house and along the lakeside for several hours, trying to justify to himself the decision he had already made not to become chairman again. He ought to agree to Velusi's idea if he felt badly about the state of things, he knew. He was being as selfish and irrational as those he despised. It was as if there were a tangible poison in the air that destroyed one's strength of mind.

Yet he could not face Velusi if it was to tell the old man that he was not going to help form a government. Perhaps he could act as a token chairman, and let Velusi do the real work? But that was no good; the people would soon realise he was not active.

He had made the right ethical decisions all his life, up

until the news of the race's sterility. First he had gone off on that wild goose chase after Orlando Sharvis, thus indirectly affecting the morale of the public, and now he was taking no pains to rectify the situation while he could.

Was there some impulse in him that was driving him to help destroy the society he valued? An impulse that had been buried since he had left the twilight region? An impulse inherited, perhaps, from his father?

Fear was encouraging the dark side of human nature to flourish again. Was it also reviving a dark side of his own nature that he had thought to be dead?

He could now sympathise to some extent, with the feelings that had led people to join the new cult. First came the fear, then the dark thoughts, then the guilt in having the thoughts. It had been a common enough syndrome in the past.

He sat down on a rock and stared into the calm water of the lake.

Perhaps he should, after all, agree to Narvo's suggestion? The practical problems of organising a new administration might divert his mind into healthier channels. He had already given in to one selfish impulse and it did not seem to have benefited anyone.

He shrugged. Very well, he would do nothing for a couple of days and then contact Narvo to say that he was ready to head a new government.

He felt more at ease as he walked back towards his house.

After he had prepared himself a light meal and eaten it, he went back up to the bedroom. Fastina was still sleeping. There was a slight smile on her lips and she seemed very much at peace. He envied her.

He took off his clothes and had a shower, then he moved desultorily around the house, sorting through his microtapes for something to look at or read, but nothing appealed to him.

A little later he got into bed beside Fastina. She stirred slightly and he put his arm around her shoulders, enjoying the sensation of her soft skin and hair against his body, feeling the old affection returning.

Soon he was also asleep.

Fastina was not beside him when he awoke, but she returned shortly with warm drinks for them both. She handed him his and came back to bed. They sipped their drinks in silence. Both were thoughtful and relaxed.

After a while he kissed her and they made love gently, handling each other carefully as if each limb was infinitely precious and fragile.

Some hours later, when they were eating breakfast on the balcony overlooking the lake, he told her what he had been doing and what he had seen. He mentioned Almer and she did not seem surprised to learn what had happened to him.

"Andros even anticipated it himself," she said. "He seemed to like the idea in a way, I think. He was always perverse."

Marca told her about Velusi's suggestion that he become chairman of a new government.

She frowned. "It would be a good idea, I suppose. It would be useful to have some sort of mediating influence between those vigilantes of Andros's and the Brotherhood. But it would take up a lot of your time, wouldn't it, Clovis? I think you ought to do as Narvo suggests—but I don't really want you to."

"I don't want to. Every instinct is against it. I'd prefer simply to retire here, or move the house to some other spot where it would be hard to find."

"Run away, Clovis? That's not like you."

"I ran away once, Fastina, when I was a child. I ran away a second time just over a year ago—though I told myself I was looking for something. I could run away a third time, couldn't I? It *is* like me . . ."

"Like all of us," she said. "Sometimes. What do you want to do, Clovis? Which impulse is strongest?"

"That's the trouble—I'm completely torn between my emotional need to keep away from it all, and my feeling that it is my duty to get involved. Oh, there are easy roads out—I could indulge in a spot of self-pity, I could argue that in the long run it all comes to the same thing—death.

71

I could build up a bit of resentment, I suppose, at their foolishness. Perhaps, eventually, I will take one of those ways out—if the situation gets worse for me. But really, if I'm to remain true to my own ideals, I must join with Narvo and form the damned government. It's partly a question of self-interest, anyway. The more power Andros gets, the more he'll want to use it—and I have the impression he doesn't feel particularly friendly towards me."

"You know why that is . . ."

"I know." He stared gloomily at the great flight of flamingoes wading in the shallows of the lake. In this timeless world of everlasting day it seemed impossible that violence and hatred could intrude and, what was more, begin to hold sway so rapidly.

"I can't help," she said.

"You don't have to. It's my problem. I'll do what I decided earlier. I'll leave it for a day or two until I feel calmer about it. Then I'll probably go and see Narvo.'"

He walked into the room, leaving the balcony. "I don't want to stay in the house, though. What shall we do?"

She joined him in the room. "We'll go to my house," she suggested, "and then we'll decide. All right?"

He sighed. "All right. A good idea. You're coddling me, Fastina. There's no need to—but it's kind of you."

"Come on," she said. "Let's go to the car."

He went up to her and hugged her. "Don't worry," he said. "I'm just off-balance at the moment, that's all."

She kissed him lightly on the chin and took his hand, leading him towards the gravishute. He followed passively, like a tired child.

He spent much longer than he had intended at her house in Greece. He took to going for protracted walks along the beach, thinking about nothing in particular. He put off contacting Narvo day after day. He dozed or slept a great deal of the time. He hardly spoke to Fastina at all but she was there whenever he was hungry or wished to make love and if she was disturbed by the remote look in his eyes, the impassive features, she kept her feelings hidden.

One day, just after he had returned from the beach, she ʌve him a drink and said: "Narvo called earlier. He ᴋed if you were here. I told him you were. He said that it ᴀs even more important than ever that you get in touch ᴛh him."

He nodded abstractedly.

"Will you contact him?" she asked.

"Yes, I'd better."

He walked slowly to the screen and spoke Velusi's ᴀme into the console. Narvo's face appeared almost im-ᴇdiately.

"I expected to hear from you earlier, Clovis. Is any-ing wrong?"

"No. I meant to talk to you, but . . ." He cleared his ᴄoat. "Why did you ask me to call you? Fastina said it ᴀs important."

"There's fighting going on, Clovis—between Almer's ᴦilantes and the Brotherhood people. Outside my house this minute!"

"What?" Marca began to feel more alert. "How did it ᴀppen?"

"The Brotherhood tried to set fire to the house. I was ʟeep. They were running about everywhere with brands ᴎen I woke up. I tried to get them to leave. They ᴏuldn't listen—they, they set hands on me—threatened ᴇ. I panicked, I'm afraid. I called Almer. Could you ᴍe over, Clovis?"

Marca nodded grimly. "Yes, of course. At once."

The fire had not really had time to get a grip on the ʟatively few things that were flammable, but the stink of ᴣrning was coming up through the gravishute as Marca ᴎded the air car on the roof.

Down the hillside, among the trees, he could see the ᴏwn-clad Brotherhood struggling with men in black, ᴏᴏded cloaks like the one he had seen Almer wearing. In ᴇ general manner of their dress, there did not seem to be ᴜch difference between the two sides.

He dropped through the gravishute and found Narvo ᴇlusi in his living room. The old man was trembling violently, sitting in his deep armchair and staring throug[h] the transparent wall at the fighting men in the woo[d] below. Velusi looked older than he had ever looked. H[is] clothes were smudged and torn, his hands dirty and blee[d] ing.

Horrified, Marca knelt down beside the chair ar[d] looked into his friend's face.

"Narvo?"

Velusi was in a state of shock. He turned his hea[d] slightly and his lips moved and even tried to smile.

The room was disordered. Furniture was overturne[d] fabric charred and water saturated the floor covering Marca had never seen such a sight at close hand. He pa[t] ted Velusi's arm and went to the wall to look out at th[e] battle.

Men were rolling about on the ground punching or[e] another. Others were using sticks torn from the trees [to] strike at one another. Marca was horrified. He touche[d] the appropriate control and the wall became blank an[d] solid again.

In the semi-darkness, he drew up a chair beside Velu[si] and sat down, trying to comfort the old man. He fetche[d] him a drink and put it into his hand.

After a while, Velusi raised the glass to his lips an[d] sipped the drink. A long, infinitely tired sigh escaped him.

"Oh, Clovis," he murmured, "I blamed you for yo[ur] apathy, but now I feel that it's not worth continuing to t[ry] to do anything. You knew it was too late, didn't you?"

"Nothing of the sort. I was just trying to come to gri[ps] with my conscience that was all. Later, when you feel be[t] ter, we'll go to the Great Glade and tell the people we i[n] tend to re-form the council."

There was a sound from behind them and a tall, blac[k] cloaked figure emerged from the gravishute. His chest w[as] rising and falling rapidly. He was dressed exactly as Alm[o] had been, save that his mask was without the scarlet edg[e] ing and his boots were black, his gloves undecorated.

He walked over to the cabinet and, unasked, pour[ed] himself a drink. He drained the glass and put it down wi[th] a thump.

"We've dealt with them," he said harshly. "I'm glad ou called us in time. This is the first real chance we've ad to have a proper go at them."

"What happened?" Marca asked hesitantly, not really anting to hear.

"We captured a couple of the maniacs. We'll put them a safe place somewhere where they can't affect anybody y more."

Marca no longer questioned the archaic terms the man sed so freely. It would not be long, he thought, before the ords 'arrest' and 'prison' would become familiar again. e felt afraid of this masked, earnest man with his brisk anner. The state of mind, reflected in the fact that he d his fellows wore uniform clothing, was one of basic security.

"Was anyone badly hurt?" Velusi asked.

"Only one of them. He is no longer with us."

"Where is he?"

"He—he is no longer with us." The masked man helped mself to another drink.

"You don't mean he's dead?" Marca got up. "You lled him?"

"If you insist on the term, yes, he's dead. There was no tention of taking his life. It was accidental. But it has its dvantages now that it's happened. It will warn the cult f from further violence . . ."

"Or incite them to vengeance," Marca said scornfully. What's happened to your education, man? Remember ur history, your psychology, your sociology!"

"The present situation is unique as you well know," the gilante replied forcefully.

"Only in one respect—certainly not in any other."

"We shall see. I must say I expected more gratitude hen I came here. We probably saved your friend's life." he man's tone was deliberately rude and there had not een quite such a breach of manners before in all Marca's xperience. He felt unable to deal with the man's im- oliteness; he had no precedent.

"This is Narvo Velusi . . ." he began.

"I know very well who he is. You are Clovis Marca.

75

I'm supposed to respect you, I gather. Well, I did once but what have you done to help the present situation Velusi has embarked upon a useless, time-wasting project with that transmitter of his—and you have done nothing at all. Very well, I accept that you are men of peace and enlightenment. Such men are not particularly useful these days. Men of action are needed—like our leader."

"Andros Almer?"

"We do not use personal names. We have dispensed with the old associations until the Brotherhood is under control. You seem ill-informed for men of affairs. Perhaps things have moved too rapidly for you—perhaps you are unused to people making rapid decisions?"

"Hasty decisions, perhaps?" Marca suggested coolly.

The man laughed harshly and turned to go. "Decisions anyway." He gestured with one gloved hand. "Look down on us from your remote height if you wish, but, if it weren't for our decisions and our action, Narvo Velusi might be badly injured, at very least, by now. You should be grateful to us. We are giving you the security to continue with your pleasant philosophising!"

"I came here today to discuss re-forming the administration," Marca told him angrily. "We intend to hold a meeting in the Great Glade today and co-opt new members on to the council."

"Noble of you. But a little belated, I would say."

The man drew his hood further over his face and entered the gravishute.

"Tell Almer we shall need him here!" Marca called after the man, half-placatingly. He realised he should have responded rather more neutrally than he had done. There was no point in angering Almer or his vigilantes. The best thing to do would be to get Almer on to the council and also, perhaps, a member of the Brotherhood cult, since it would be only fair to have all sides represented.

He smiled ironically, then.

When, in the past, had such attempted conciliation worked when the parties concerned were so full of anger and distrust?

CHAPTER TWO

Men of Judgement

As soon as the meeting began, Marca realised that it was all but useless. The proportion of black-cloaked vigilantes and brown-habited cult members in the auditorium was slightly higher than the proportion of ordinary men and women. He had not realised how quickly groups of that sort could grow.

Hovering above, in their black air cars, were several more of Almer's vigilantes. Almer himself sat on the platform with Narvo Velusi and Marca. He leaned back casually, with his arms folded and his legs crossed: the very picture of arrogance. His hood was flung back, but he wore his mask still.

Looking around the auditorium, Marca saw that the fashion for wearing masks—albeit brightly coloured ones—had also increased. There were scarcely twenty people there who did not wear a mask of some kind.

Velusi had recovered. His hands were still bruised and his shoulders were not held as straight as normal, but he gave the appearance of being relaxed. He stood up to open the meeting.

"As you have heard," he began, "Clovis Marca has agreed to head a new administration which will be specifically concerned with dealing with the various problems that have arisen since the old council disbanded."

He was speaking very carefully, Marca thought, making sure he offended no one.

"The new administration," Velusi continued, "will attempt to insure that people will have security and perhaps, a sense of purpose . . ."

He went on in this vein for some time, but Marca could tell that Velusi's diplomatic words were making no impression at all. The Brotherhood of Guilt was fanatical and convinced of their own right to act as they saw fit. The vigilantes evidently despised the kind of argument Velusi was using. As for the ordinary people, they could look around them and see how useless it was to try to reconcile the opposed groups by means of placatory words.

"And so we require volunteers," Velusi concluded. "Preferably people who have served on a council of some kind in the past. Would those willing raise their hands?"

All the Brotherhood members raised their hands. Most of the vigilantes raised their hands. Two ordinary people raised their hands, glanced about, and lowered them again.

Marca realised that a mockery was being made of the whole anarchic-democratic system they had lived by for so long.

The idea of forming a new administration on a sane and rational basis had been doomed from the start, it was now plain. Perhaps he had instinctively realised this and for that reason had been slow to act?

Velusi was evidently at a loss.

"Perhaps if you could remove your masks . . ." he began.

Marca got up. He thought he heard Almer chuckle from where he sat, still in the same casual posture.

"We want a balanced representation," said Marca as levelly as he could. "Could we have a few more volunteers from the—" he pretended to smile—"non-aligned men and women here?"

No more hands were raised.

Suddenly there was a scream from above them. Everyone looked into the air. A black-cloaked man was falling towards the ground. He landed with a smack just short of the platform. Marca rushed towards him but he could tell from the way the body lay that he was dead. He egan to peel off the mask, to see who it was.

The man seemed to have fallen from his air car, yet he was wearing a gravstrap. It had not been switched on.

He heard a shout. People were still looking upwards.

There, drifting away from the air car on a gravstrap, was a brown-habited member of the Brotherhood.

It was evident that he had come up behind the vigilante and pushed him out of his car before he could operate his gravstrap.

Vigilantes were now rising into the air to give chase, others were grappling with Brotherhood members in the iers of the auditorium.

Marca still had his hand on the dead man's mask and now he felt someone touch his shoulder. He looked up into the shadowed face of Andros Almer.

"Don't remove his mask," Almer said icily. "Didn't you know that was one of the reasons for wearing them—so we shall not know who are dead and who are living?"

Marca straightened and stood looking at Almer.

"This is superstition, Andros!"

"Is it? We think it is practical." There was a triumphant, bantering note in Almer's voice now. "We are a practical group of men. It was a worthy decision to make, Clovis, about forming a government, but as you can see it is unnecessary. I suggest you and Narvo go home and stay out of all this. We can look after things perfectly well."

Marca looked to where a great mass of men were fighting. The whole auditorium was in confusion. In the air two cars crashed head on with a great splintering sound. Men dropped out of them and began fighting in mid-air.

"As you can see, there is too much violence for a man like yourself to cope with, Clovis." Almer said patronisingly, with soft amusement. "There's a new order now—one well-equipped to deal with this sort of thing. I would rather see you safely away from the unpleasantness . ."

Marca felt the anger coming back with renewed strength. He wanted to strike Almer.

"You helped produce this situation, Andros—you are doing nothing to get rid of it! Look what happened earlier.

Your men killed a Brotherhood member. Now a Brotherhood member kills one of your men. You can only make things worse!"

"We shall see."

As Narvo Velusi and Clovis Marca flew back towards their air car, a voice from below cried *"Cowards!"*

Bewildered and outraged by the turn of events, the two men headed towards Fastina's house on the Greek coast, hurrying away from the noise and confusion in the Great Glade.

They flew over the flower forest. Its heavy scents and richly coloured flowers half-surprised them as they looked down.

"There is nothing we can do, after all." Velusi said after a while. "That was the defeat of reason you saw back there—symbolised and displayed."

Marca nodded.

"What do we do now, Narvo?"

"I don't know. Stay out of it for a while. What else can we do?"

"It depends what happens," Marca said. "For how long will Almer confine himself to fighting only the Brotherhood? When will he begin to arrest those he suspects of being 'secret' members? There is even the chance that the Brotherhood will get the upper hand and destroy him and his vigilantes. It would not matter."

"At least Almer speaks for order," Velusi said.

"Of a sort," Marca agreed. "But there will be no difference between them in a short while."

"I suppose not." Velusi seemed no longer interested His voice was heavy with despair.

"Perhaps we should take Almer's advice and stay out of things," Marca said. "It's not our world now, Narvo—it's becoming unrecognisable. Let them sort out their own problems."

Velusi nodded.

A little later the old man said: "We can ignore them Clovis, easily enough. But will they ignore us?"

A month later, lying on the white beach, half submerged in the warm sea, Clovis Marca heard the thump of someone running towards him.

It was Fastina. He stretched out a hand to her, smiling, but she shook her head. "It's the news, Clovis. Narvo said you'd want to see it."

She began to run back and he followed her more slowly.

Velusi was hunched forward, watching the laser-screen on which, lately, news bulletins had begun to be broadcast. The screens had not been used for such things since Central Information had been set up to serve anyone who wished to know something. But information was now restricted and channelised into the regular hourly bulletins operated from the old Central Information building, which was under the control of Almer's vigilantes.

The scene on the screen showed the Great Glade. The glade was now surrounded by a force wall nearly a mile high. This was to restrict passage to and from it.

On the enlarged platform stood three members of the Brotherhood. They had been stripped naked, but their shaven heads were sufficient to tell what they were. Two were men and one was a woman. They were dirty and there were recent scars on their bodies. By the look of them, they could hardly stand with exhaustion and starvation.

Black-cloaked vigilantes ringed the platform. They all bore swords in their hands; long blades of bright steel. So far these were the only weapons that had been manufactured, but in a world otherwise without weapons, they were sufficient to suit the vigilantes' purpose.

In a high chair, raised above the floor of the platform, sat a man who could be recognised as Almer by his red boots and scarlet-trimmed mask and gloves.

He was not called Almer now, by his men, but simply 'leader'.

Almer's voice came from the laser-screen.

"I judge you guilty of complicity in the murder of another citizen," Almer was saying. "And sentence you to die so that your fellows will learn by your example."

"No!" Marca looked incredulously at his friends. "Has it reached this stage already?"

"I said it would be rapid," Velusi said tonelessly. "In a society not equipped to withstand this sort of thing, people like Almer and his vigilantes can develop as quickly as they wish to."

Marca saw the ring of vigilantes turn inwards, their swords raised.

The Brotherhood people fell to their knees, making no attempt to resist.

The swords fell, rose, and fell again, sparkling with blood in the strong sunlight.

Then the vigilantes stepped back from the corpses.

They had been butchered beyond recognition.

Marca controlled his need to vomit. He could not move to switch off the set, but watched in fascination as Almer stepped haughtily down from his chair and stood near the bloody pile of flesh and bone.

Almer looked down at it for a moment and then disdainfully drew in his cloak and walked around it, leaving the platform and crossing to a specially cleared space in the auditorium where his black air car stood guarded by four of his men.

The auditorium, Marca could now see, was packed.

CHAPTER THREE

Men of Conscience

After that, they switched off the laser-screen for good. They moved the house from Greece to the deep jungles of Ceylon, close to Anuradhapura, the ancient city of the Mahavansa, with its great domes and ziggurats dating from almost five hundred years before the Christian era. Thousands of years old, the buildings had survived tidal waves and earthquakes and the encroachment of the jungle. No one lived there now. No one visited the city. They could site the house in the shade of a temple, disguise it with tree branches, and be invisible from the air.

Months passed and they found comparative happiness in the jungle city. It was everlasting afternoon, mild and golden. Monkeys and brightly coloured birds moved through the foliage and over the old, vine-covered stones of the buildings. Jungle and city seemed merged into one ancient entity.

Occasionally Narvo Velusi would take the air car and go to the Black Sea to supervise work on his transmitter. Almost a colony had formed there, he told the others, of people who wanted nothing to do with Almer or the Brotherhood. He would bring back extra supplies every time he visited the transmitter and once he made a point of calling on Brand Calax, who had not been bothered by the Brotherhood since Almer had come to power and had been full of praise for the vigilantes' system.

One day, when they were picnicking on the grassy slope of a ziggurat, they saw an air car come drifting down through the trees. Instinctively they looked for cover, but then Velusi recognised the carriage.

"It's Brand. He asked where we were and I had to tell him. He promised he would keep the secret."

They knew that if anyone really wished to seek them out it could be done systematically, using instruments, but they hoped that the old maxim 'out of sight, out of mind' would hold true as far as Almer or the Brotherhood were concerned. They were simply being cautious, they told themselves.

Brand guided his car down until he was hovering beside them.

"I tried to get you on the screen," he said, "but I couldn't get through. So I thought I'd come personally and say goodbye."

He was paler and gaunter still, but he seemed very cheerful.

"The ship is complete, is it?" Marca said. Like the other two, he wore only a loose kilt around his middle and he was very brown.

"Yes. We blast off tomorrow. I'll be back in six months of course . . ."

"Of course," said Marca.

". . . and I shouldn't wonder if I won't have a couple of healthy Titanians with me in *The Orlando Sharvis.*"

Velusi, who still did not know that Marca had already been to Titan, said slowly: "Are you sure you'll manage the voyage both ways, Brand?"

Calax laughed. "Surer than ever. I'll make you all eat your words when I come back."

Fastina smiled. "You'll do a lot of good if you do find some Titanians, Brand." The smile trembled and her expression was pitying before she turned her head away, pretending to pack up the picnic things. Calax had not noticed her face and he grinned. "I know it."

He brought the air car a little closer, so that they could climb aboard. "I hope you'll offer me a drink to celebrate. You guide me, and I'll take you back to your home."

In the main room, which was full of the golden-green

light of the forest, Calax sat down and stretched his legs.

"You know, I'm in agreement with a lot that Almer's doing. He's got strength and conviction and he knows what he wants to do. A few people have got hurt, I realise, but it was no more than they deserved. I can't understand his constant antipathy towards my Titan project. It's such a negative attitude for such a positive man to hold."

"I would have said his whole attitude was negative," Fastina said, leaning against the transparent wall and looking at the trees which grew right up to the house. They were gnarled old trees and had probably been there since before the raid.

"I don't see that," Calax told her. He looked back at Marca and Velusi who were standing together behind his chair. "And I don't understand why you're hiding from him like this. What harm would he do you? He's only interested in controlling the madmen who've joined this cult. I know he's had to take emergency measures to check the thing growing and so on, and I don't say he has to kill these people, but someone like him was needed. He filled a demand, you know. He was what everyone but the Brotherhood wanted."

"Yes," said Velusi, "you're probably right. But better safe than sorry, eh?"

"He won't try to do anything to people like you—ex-members of the council! He wouldn't dare for one thing, and he wouldn't need to for another. I just don't know why you're worrying."

"Neither do we," Marca put in. "Just call it the example of history. We're probably being over-pessimistic. But when a man like Almer goes insane, anything that conflicts with his view of things is likely to be regarded as a threat."

"Almer insane? He's not insane, Clovis. He follows his fashion of masking and so on, and maybe he's a bit more brutal than he should be, but that's not insanity—not strictly."

Velusi laughed. The laugh was a little strained. "Let's not argue any more. We should be drinking to the success of your trip, Brand."

After Calax had left, the three of them sat in the room looking at the monkeys playing over the half-ruined temple. They chattered and squawked, knocking one another from their perches, leaping wildly from level to level and from stone to stone.

As they watched the monkeys they began to relax and smile.

"I think I'll re-connect the laser-screen tomorrow," Marca said, "just to see Brand taking off. I don't think he'll be back."

"There's a chance," Velusi said.

"I don't think so." Marca got up. "When he finds that there's no human colony on Titan, I don't think he'll want to come back. I think he knows there isn't a chance. He wants to go there to die, that's my guess."

"He could die just as easily here if he wanted to kill himself," Fastina said.

"That's not the point. He wants to die trying—doing something. You can't blame him."

When he and Fastina went to bed that night, their love-making was cruel and desperate.

The next day they sat down to watch the take-off on the laser-screen. It was not being covered on Almer's official broadcasts, but there were cameras trained on the ship. The cameras were of the ordinary domestic kind, but they were sufficient to show the mountain valley and the great steel ship ready on its launching pad.

There was no commentary, no count-down that they could hear, as the ship began to warm up.

The ship was built to a design that was nowadays unusual. It was a slender, tapering thing, with circular fins at its base.

Its drive began to murmur, its hull began to tremble slightly, and then it was rising slowly into the air.

They said nothing as they watched *The Orlando Sharvis* climb upwards, beginning to gather speed; but they gasped when the explosion came.

The whole hull burst apart in blue and orange flames.

Pieces of the ship were flung in all directions and they saw them begin to fall while the antigravity drive unit continued alone to sail upwards, as if unaware that the ship it had powered had broken into a thousand fragments.

They heard the roar of the explosion and the screen rattled and reverberated as its speakers were unable to take the strain. They could almost feel the heat of the blast.

"Sabotaged," whispered Fastina. "It must have been."

"But by whom?" Velusi was badly shaken. "Who killed him?"

The scene faded and a masked member of the vigilantes appeared on the screen.

"We have just received news that Brand Calax's Titan ship, *The Orlando Sharvis,* has blown up," said the man. "It is suspected that members of the - notorious Brotherhood of Guilt or their sympathisers were responsible for this destruction. Brand Calax, the heroic ex-Warden of Ganymede who was embarking on a lone expedition to seek survivors of the rumoured Titan colony . . ."

"Too quick," Marca said. "What do you say, Narvo?"

The old man nodded. "They were expecting it. They knew it was going to happen. They're the ones who did it. Almer did not want Calax to build the ship in the first place. I thought it was strange that he didn't interfere with him. They sabotaged the ship, unquestionably."

". . . those responsible will be found and punished," the vigilante was saying. "This is perhaps the worst crime the so-called Brotherhood has yet committed. Be certain, however, that we shall protect you against further outrages of this kind."

"They don't need further outrages," Fastina said. "And there can't be anything like it. Why has Almer done this?"

"Probably for several reasons," Velusi murmured, "to consolidate his own position because he probably wants a reason for extending his power, to make the people even more reliant on him than they are already, to punish Brand Calax for his 'obstinacy' and not listening to 'reason' . . . The man's clever and psychotic at once. The combination is pretty rare, by all accounts." Velusi shook his head sorrowfully. "Poor, Brand—he wanted to die, but not like that."

"I'm going to see him," Marca said suddenly.

Velusi did not take him seriously. "What good would that do?"

"He still has his conscience. He still has to justify these actions to himself."

"He's too far gone—he can justify anything now."

"I might as well try, anyway. And I might get the chance to see Yoluf at Central Information. He would possibly give me a chance to broadcast the truth. This can't go on unchecked . . ."

"You think you can check him now? We tried and failed. Now he has more power than ever."

Fastina broke in. "It would be dangerous, Clovis. Don't go."

"I'm afraid of him, Fastina—as we all are. I must try to face him nonetheless."

Velusi shook his head. "We must be more subtle, Clovis. The only thing we could do would be to get together a group of our own and undermine Almer's power gradually."

"While he murders at will?"

Velusi sighed. "Very well, go to see him, but be on your guard, Clovis."

CHAPTER FOUR

Men of Reason

Almer's headquarters were in the old Main Administration Building just south of the flower forest that enclosed the Great Glade. Though still surrounded by its smooth lawns, it seemed to have been turned into a fortress, guarded by vigilantes armed with swords and a forcefield that was partially visible; the shimmering air that indicated its presence gave it extra menace.

Strangest of all, a flag flew from the roof of the building. The letter 'V' had been worked on it and beneath this were the smaller words 'For Order'. The V could stand for vigilante or even, Marca guessed, for some dead-language word, like Vita. Although not personally familiar with such things, he had seen enough similar examples in his history tapes.

Well before he had reached the force barrier an amplified voice roared from a phonoplate close by.

"Stop! It's forbidden to approach Main Admin by air!"

Marca stopped the car as two vigilantes on gravstraps came speeding up from the ground. They dropped into his car and stood looking down at him. He rose, frowning.

"I have come to see An—your leader," he said. "Tell him that Clovis Marca is here." He spoke with deliberate firmness.

They both seemed to relax a trifle then and one of them spoke apparently into the air. Marca knew that his voice was picked up by the tiny earbead transceiver in his ear. The man relayed Marca's message and then waited for a reply.

Marca stood there impatiently for several minutes until at length the vigilante looked up and said: "It's all right. They'll make an opening in the screen. Go through carefully—the thing's charged with enough energy to stun you badly."

The two men left his air car and returned to the ground. Marca saw a gap appear in the screen well above the level of the lawn and he guided his air car through it to land on the roof of the building.

Two more guards were waiting for him there. They were swathed, like the others, in their heavy black hoods and cloaks, but their masks and gloves were edged in yellow braid. This was evidently some sign of rank or function. This evidence of further erosion of individuality depressed Marca. He let them lead him to the gravishaft.

They fell several storeys and then entered what had once been the big council meeting room. Where there had been seats for almost a hundred people, there was now only one chair at the far end near the darkened wall. It was the same black, high-backed chair that Marca had seen on his laser-screen several months before when Almer had had his men murder the Brotherhood members. The chair was equipped with an antigravity generator, for it hovered about a foot off the floor.

The walls were now lined with scores of laser-screens and just in front of Almer's chair was a console that evidently controlled them.

Almer sat in the chair, even more arrogant in posture than ever. He signalled to the guards and they left.

Marca faced Almer alone.

He began to walk down towards the masked man.

When he had covered half the distance, Almer drawled: "No further please, Clovis."

Marca stopped, puzzled. "Why is that?"

"I have enemies. It is impossible to trust anyone. Besides, after today's wanton murder of Brand Calax and the destruction of his ship . . ."

"That's what I came to see you about."

"You know, perhaps, which members of the
90

Brotherhood were responsible?" Almer's tone was sardonic.

"I know that they were not responsible."

"Oh? Then who was it?" Almer crossed his legs and settled deeper in his chair. "You? Have you come to confess, Clovis?"

"You were responsible, Andros. It was quite plain—your news bulletin came too rapidly and too fluently after the explosion . . ."

"Did it now? We live and learn. Thank you, Clovis."

"All these lies! This myth you are building! Your evasion of reality, both personally and publicly, is almost unbelievable, Andros. You hide in your hoods and masks, you hide in half-baked ideas, you hide, now, in outright lies. For your own sake, listen to me!"

"I'm listening," said Almer banteringly.

"There comes a point in a situation like this where you become so far removed from actuality that your own system of lies defeats you. It has happened often enough in the past. Your lie becomes your reality—but it is only yours. You begin to operate according to a set of self-formulated laws that conflict with the actual laws of existence. If you continue, you will realise that eventually. But if you listen to me now, you will be able to rectify the position and . . ."

Almer began to laugh. "Thank you, Clovis, thank you. What a sweet-hearted man you are. You come to save me from myself, eh?"

"I suppose so."

"Oh, Clovis, don't you see that it doesn't matter about my reality and the reality any more? We have only so long to live. We can do what we like. I can play kings here—you can play hermits wherever you've hidden yourself. We are both in hiding—but you hide in your detachment while I hide in my *attachment.*"

"I don't see . . ."

"Yes you do, yes you do. You hide by refusing to become involved in all this—I hide, if you like, by involving myself in it up to the chin. More than that, Clovis, I

91

act as the catalyst, do you see? I cause things to happen that much faster!" Andros began to laugh again.

"You aren't as insane as I thought you were," Clovis said quietly. "Or at least . . ."

"I know I am? Is that what you want to say?"

"It will do."

Almer chuckled. "You don't have to tell me that this process will result in mutual destruction eventually. But I am following the rules, Clovis. I am doing all the things I should. I am repressive. I aggravate a situation by publicly murdering people. I sabotage spaceships. I lie and distort the truth and then arrest people on false charges." He leaned forward, still smiling. "And I wait to see how far I can go before some resistance is offered by thoughtful people like yourself, Clovis . . ."

"You expected me here?"

"Sooner or later. I've been disappointed on the whole—I expected opposition earlier. My public killings were actually popular. I had underestimated the people. I had underestimated the power of fear."

"So I am here. And obviously I cannot appeal to you to stop."

"I have anticipated all your arguments, I believe."

"All but one. Haven't we a duty to help people lead happier lives than these?"

"Duty? I am no Messiah, Clovis. But you are, perhaps?" Andros Almer's tone not only mocked him but somehow struck an unpleasant chord deep inside Marca. He began to wish very much that he had not come to see Almer.

"You are an arrogant man, Andros Almer."

"Arrogant? Arrogant? Oh, come now, Clovis!"

"You imply that I'm arrogant . . ."

"Aren't you? Clovis—I am merely moving with the tide of events."

"And turning them to your advantage."

"Someone would have done. You, under other circumstances, perhaps?"

"Perhaps."

"Well, then?"

Marca shrugged. "I left things too late. If I had stayed . . ."

"Things might be the same today—only you would be sitting in this fine chair." Almer slapped the arm.

"I don't think so."

"Maybe not. But they would be the same tomorrow or the next day. You are slower to accept the obvious, that's all."

"I like to think you're wrong, Andros," Marca sighed. "But I suppose it is possible that I would have found myself forced into the position you now occupy. I did anticipate that—and that was one of the reasons I chose to do nothing until too late."

"There you are then!"

A signal on one of the central laser-screens had been blinking urgently for some moments. Almer had ignored it up to now. He drifted in his chair to the console and reached out a gloved hand to touch a stud.

A masked and hooded vigilante appeared on the screen.

"About twenty suspects have been rounded up, leader," said the man. "Half are actual Brotherhood members and the rest are thought to be secret sympathisers."

"They are the ones on the list I gave you?" Almer asked.

"Most of them. We still have to locate one or two."

"Good work. Find them soon."

Marca shook his head. "I take it these are people you regard as dangerous. You intend to accuse them of destroying the spaceship?"

"Quite so." Almer turned his attention back to the vigilante who was still on the screen. "And the other matter? How is that progressing?"

"We expect the result very soon, leader."

"Excellent!"

The man faded from the screen.

"What 'other matter'?" Marca asked.

"Oh, I expect you will hear of it shortly," Almer told him. "Now, Clovis. I must supervise the questioning of our suspects. If there is nothing else . . . ?"

"Plainly there is nothing I can do?"

"Certainly there is nothing you can *say,* Clovis, that will affect me. Goodbye."

Marca turned and went to the gravishute entrance. The guards were still there, hovering just inside. They escorted him back to the roof.

Almer's last statement seemed to have been something of a challenge.

As Marca flew back towards Ceylon, he let the golden air car drift slowly while he tried to gather his thoughts. Almer seemed to want him to take some sort of positive action against the vigilantes and Almer himself. In short, Almer wanted to fight Marca, perhaps to test himself and almost certainly to 'win' Fastina from his rival.

Marca had no intention in playing this game, but Almer might try to force him to in some way. Almer had impressed Marca with one thing; the man could only be brought down by violent means now.

Marca was still horrified at the idea of using violence and yet could think of no subtle method.

About half-an-hour after he had left Almer's fortress, he glanced behind him and noticed several flying objects coming closer. They were probably air cars and they were moving very rapidly. Soon they could be seen plainly. There were five black air cars, and standing in them, their cloaks billowing out behind them, were vigilantes.

Marca frowned. Was Almer already trying to force his hand?

The cars caught up with him and began to surround him and Marca saw the men draw the straight swords with which they were all armed.

"What's going on?" he called.

"We have been ordered to take you into custody, Clovis Marca!" one of them shouted back. "Turn your car about and come with us."

"What is the reason?"

"Suspicion of complicity in sabotage."

"Oh, this is stupid. I was nowhere near Calax's spaceship for months. Even Almer can't make that sound right!"

94

"The charge is not connected with the Titan ship. You are thought to have helped sabotage the giant radio transmitter project initiated by Narvo Velusi."

Now Marca knew what the other matter was that Almer had mentioned earlier.

"You have destroyed Velusi's transmitter, is that it?" he said levelly. "You are contemptible."

"Come with us."

Marca touched the control that operated the car's forceshield and instantly the car was enclosed in an invisible bubble of force. The vigilantes did not seem to have noticed this action. Marca felt in his pocket and took out the ultrasonic whistle there, trying to remember the code he needed. He had never had occasion to use it before.

One of the vigilantes gestured impatiently with his sword and his voice was muffled now by the screen.

"We are prepared to use violence if you do not come willingly," he said.

Marca took the whistle from his pocket and blew three long blasts on it.

The car began to hurtle upwards and he was flung to the couch as it went into an emergency climb. If he had not been protected by the screen, Marca could not have survived the rapid ascent into the ionosphere. As it was the only air he had was that trapped inside the bubble.

He looked down. The cars were climbing very slowly it seemed.

His chest felt sore and he could hardly get to his feet again. He looked out over the planet, searching for what he needed. Then he saw them. A group of cumulus clouds to his west. If he could dive into them, he might stand a chance of evading the vigilantes.

The clouds were travelling in roughly the same direction he had been going before the vigilantes turned up.

He settled himself back into a couch and felt under the ledge of the car to find the manually operated control board. He swung it out and his fingers moved over the studs, giving the car its directions.

The car dipped and began to dive, like the huge bird it resembled.

95

Marca was again pressed deep into the cushions as the car hurtled downwards. He could not see if the vigilantes were following him.

Then he was in the obscuring mist of the clouds. He quickly cut the car's speed and calculated the speed at which the clouds were travellng.

Gently, he began to move along, using the clouds as a cover.

He would have to wait and see if the vigilantes had discovered his trick.

Several hours later, Marca knew that it had worked. He had been forced to switch off the screen and let the cold, clammy mist into the car, but it was the only way he could breathe.

The quality of the light told him that he was entering the twilight region and he judged that it was safe to leave the clouds and descend into the warmer air.

Dropping from the clouds, he saw that he was over the ocean and he guessed that it was probably the Bay of Bengal. He checked his instruments and set his course for Ceylon, travelling rapidly.

Soon the island was in sight and he swept lower and lower over the jungles until he could make out the buildings of Anuradhapura below.

With a feeling of relief, he circled into the jungle, guiding the car among the trees to land on the mosaic roof of the house.

There were two other air cars already there. They were black and they were familiar. He was sure that one of them was Andros Almer's.

Panic-stricken, Marca dashed for the gravishute. It now seemed likely that the attempt to arrest him had been designed to keep him away from the house while Almer and some of his vigilantes went there. Perhaps the vigilantes had even let him escape.

He dropped into the shaft and drifted down to the entrance of the main room. He could hear voices. He reached out and grabbed the hand-grip, hanging there and peering cautiously into the room.

Almer only had two others with him. They were holding Fastina who was struggling.

Almer himself stood over Narvo Velusi. There was a sword in Almer's hand and there was blood on the sword.

It took Marca a while to realise the truth that Velusi was in fact dead and that Almer was his murderer.

Almer was chuckling. "If that doesn't force Marca to do something desperate, nothing will." He turned to Fastina who looked away from him in disgust. "It's quite traditional, really, Fastina. Now we take you off with us—and the noble prince has to rescue the fair princess from the wicked baron." He laughed again. "What a game!"

Marca was trembling with rage as he entered the room, unseen as yet by any of them.

Then he flung himself at Andros Almer, grabbing him clumsily around the throat with one arm and punching at his body with his free fist.

Almer shouted and tried to release himself. Marca was weeping as he punched. Almer's sword fell to the floor as he turned and began to grapple with Marca.

One of the men let go of Fastina and came forward, drawing his sword. Marca managed to swing Almer round so that the vigilante leader formed a shield between himself and the other swordsman, but Almer twisted away and broke free.

For a little while they stood there, panting and glaring at one another. Almer's man seemed uncertain what to do and kept looking to his leader for instructions.

Marca dived for the fallen sword, picked it up and aimed an awkward blow at Almer who skipped aside.

Marca found himself confronting the other swordsman. He had no idea how to use the weapon he had in his hand and knew that he had no chance against the vigilante who was now beginning to edge around him, crouched and feinting. There was a smile on Almer's face now.

"I'll have your blade," he told his man. "This really will be quite dramatic."

Almer took the sword from the vigilante and clashed it

lightly against Marca's. He half turned his head, his smile broadening, and spoke to Fastina who was looking on, her expression tragic.

"There's a bargain, Fastina," Almer said. "He who wins this duel shall have your hand. What do you say?"

She said nothing. She knew there was nothing to say which would make Almer stop.

Marca now held his sword out clumsily before him, backing away as Almer advanced.

Almer grinned and lunged, pulling the point of his sword just short of Marca's heart. Marca had made a defensive movement with his sword, but it would have been too late to save him if Almer had been in earnest. He swung the sword out in an arc, slashing at Almer who leapt lightly backwards.

"You haven't the same interest in these romantic old customs, Clovis—if you had, you would stand a better chance."

He thrust again with the sword and again Marca parried it too late. Grinning, Almer moved his sword from side to side as Marca tried to return a lunge. Marca knew that Almer was going to kill him eventually.

He lowered the sword.

"You will have to butcher me as you butchered Narvo," he said quietly. "I still refuse to play your game, Andros."

Almer assumed an expression of mock disappointment.

"Oh, Clovis—where's your sense of fun?"

"When you have killed me, what do you intend to do with Fastina?"

Almer put his masked head on one side, his eyes gleaming from behind the cloth.

"What does a villain always do? He *rapes* and he *humiliates* and then he *slays!*" He chuckled as he saw Marca raise the sword again. "That's better, Clovis. That's better."

Slashing wildly, Marca attacked and then, quite suddenly, the sword was gone from his hand. Almer had twisted it away.

Almer was grinning no longer. Hatred was there now as he drew back his sword arm to finish Marca.

There was a movement from behind them and a new figure could be seen standing in the gravishute. He held an object in his hand, a bulbous instrument from which extended a tube. Marca thought he recognised it. It was probably a gun. Almer lowered his sword.

"Who are you?" one of the vigilantes said.

"My name is Mr. Take. This thing in my hand is a weapon. It fires a poison charge which kills as soon as it touches any part of your body. It will be my pleasure to use it unless you release Clovis Marca and the girl at once."

"A gun! Where did you get a gun?" Almer took a step forward, staring at the object.

"I have had it for a very long time. I am a soldier—or was once. This is one of many guns of all kinds I had."

One of the vigilantes sneered. "He's mad. We haven't made any guns yet ourselves. I'll soon . . ." He lunged at Take with his sword. Take's hand moved abnormally fast. There was a brief hissing sound, the vigilante groaned, clutched his chest and fell to the floor.

"A gun, as I said," Take continued. "I have no feelings of mercy for you, Andros Almer. I will kill you without reluctance if you do not obey. Throw that sword thing down."

The sword clattered to the floor. Marca and Fastina moved to join Take at the gravishute entrance.

Almer shouted: "I'll find you! Where are you from?"

"Titan," Take replied as he followed Marca and Fastina up towards the roof.

CHAPTER FIVE

Men of Vision

Take took them away in Fastina's golden bird-shaped air car, heading East.

All were silent; Take because he was concentrating on the instruments and Marca and Fastina because they were too stunned by recent events.

Gradually, the light began to change in quality as they crossed the Bay of Bengal and left the sun behind.

Below, the water darkened to deep blue, reflecting the red rays of the sun. The air car cast a long, black shadow ahead and the sky was full of rich, hazy yellows, reds and purples.

Marca spoke, eventually, in a low voice, "Where are we going?"

"We're going home, Clovis Marca." Take's own tone was as vibrant and deep as it had been when they had first confronted each other in the house at Lake Tanganyika.

Land was ahead; the coastline of Burma. The dark jungles of the twilight were soon beneath them and from time to time they passed over the ruins of cities, mysterious in the perpetual half light. Sometimes, too, they saw a tower standing alone in a clearing. The towers looked as if they had been formed of molten rock that had cooled so that it was impossible to tell if they were natural or man-made. They were familiar to Marca, for he had been born in one.

Take changed course slightly and began to drop lower. Marca now recognised the land area as the region where once the borders of Burma, China and Thailand had met.

Now Take was heading north, towards the country that had once been Mongolia, and Marca realised what Take had meant.

"We're going to my father's house, is that it?"

"Yes."

"Why?"

"You will be safe there. You know the house."

"Of course!" Marca said. "The defences."

"Exactly."

All the old towers had defences, though there had never been any use for them. It was just one effect of the introverted character of the twilight people who had hidden thmselves in their towers and taken every possible precaution to see that they were never disturbed.

It was quite true that they would be safe there, even if Almer followed them, for the armaments of the tower would still be in working condition and could be used to repel any attack Almer could make.

Soon the landscape below changed from forests to mountains and then to desert.

Red dust and brown lichen were now all that could be seen for miles. A light, cool wind blew over the desert, rustling the lichen, stirring the dust; and then a tower came into sight.

The tower was tall and bulky, and though its materials were primarily of steel and a kind of fibreglass, it, like the other towers they had passed, had the appearance of a strange volcanic rock formation. Darkly shining greens and yellows merged with gulleys of orange and blue and thin frozen bubbles of pink covered the openings of windows. There were no straight lines or angles in the building. Everything flowed and spread and curved like living matter that had suddenly petrified. There was no symmetry to the tower. Even the main doorway was an irregular shape, rather like a crudely drawn letter G on its side, resembling the entrance to some undersea grotto.

Take landed the air car. Fastina shivered as she looked around at the dead landscape and the looming, twisted tower that was illuminated by the mellow sunlight.

"Only you can open the tower, I believe," said Take.

"How do you know that?" Marca asked as they trod across the soft, sighing dust towards the entrance.

"I know a great deal about you," Take said.

Marca had begun to notice that Take's voice was always deep and vibrant and that the basic tone never changed so that while the voice was pleasant, it was also almost expressionless.

They reached the entrance. It was protected by a sheet of smooth material that looked like a thin membrane but was actually impervious to anything that tried to destroy it. Only Marca's touch on it could make it ripple downwards to the ground.

Marca touched the warm membrane and it responded at once. The entrance was open.

They walked through.

Marca put his arm around Fastina's shoulders and stretched out his free hand to touch the stud to re-awake the tower's heating and lighting system.

Faint, yellow light now filled the passage that seemed walled by dark, veined crystal. The light actually came from the iridescent sides, roof and floor of the passage. Behind them, at Marca's activation, the membrane once more rose to close the entrance.

They stepped from the passage into an oddly shaped room with a roof that slanted close to the floor at the far end, the walls also emitting light which was, this time, milky yellow in keeping with the opalescent walls.

Two low, oval passages led from this room. The passages had walls of a soft, pinkish colour. The furniture of the whitish room was as asymmetrical as the rest of the tower and took odd forms. Here a chair was designed to look like a crouching gargoyle with open arms, there a table resembled a kneeling, grinning beast with a broad flat back.

The grotesque, half-barbaric ornamentation of the tower so contrasted with the simplicity of the daylight houses, that Fastina was obviously finding it hard to get used to the place. The design everywhere as they wandered through the upper parts of the tower, was like the brilliant imaginings of a certain kind of surrealist painter;

morbid, yet moving, fantastic, but inspired. Not one room looked the same. All were contorted to resemble nothing so much as the innards of an animal, save that every room had its particular colour, though all the walls resembled silicon or crystal.

In a top room Marca found the controls for the tower's armament. In keeping with the rest of the place, the control panel was ornate, in beaten brass and heavily worked gold and silver. Each individual control was in the form of a fierce fantastic beast's head and the instruments were arranged to look like eyes and open mouths, with dials, meters and indicators inset.

He found a book beside the panel, written in his father's hand. It was a manual for operating the force-screens, laser-cannon, energy-guns and other armament both offensive and defensive.

He worked the controls and saw the panel registering activation all over the tower. The defences were in good order.

Take and Fastina were watching him from near the doorway.

"All the towers in the twilight region are similarly equipped," Take said, his voice reverberating through the place. "If anyone wished to oppose Almer they would have a great arsenal at their disposal. Almer could not match it. It would take too long to redevelop weapons on this scale."

"Are you suggesting I use this stuff to carry a war into the daylight region?" Marca asked.

"Not at all, Clovis Marca. My comment was merely a comment, nothing more."

"What was your purpose in rescuing us, then?" Fastina asked. She looked a little less pale now.

"None, other than that I knew how much Clovis Marca valued life. I have been watching you in Anuradhapura, you know, for some time. I saw the black-cloaked ones arrive, I saw Clovis Marca arrive. It occurred to me that you would be in danger, so I came to help."

"Why have you been watching?" Marca asked. There was no anger in his question, only curiosity now.

"I was not sure that you had given up your earlier quest."

"The one for Orlando Sharvis?" Fastina said.

Take nodded. His head still lolled slightly, as if kept up by an effort.

"What would you have done if I had taken up the search again?" Marca asked.

"If you had got close to him, I should have killed you." Take replied.

"And yet you saved our lives . . . ?" Fastina began.

"So Orlando Sharvis does still exist!" Marca's tone was eager.

"I saved your lives," Take agreed, "but I would have killed Clovis Marca to save him from something else—from Sharvis."

"Where is Sharvis?" Marca left the control panel and approached Take. "On Titan? You said you were from Titan . . ."

"I am, in a sense," Take answered, "but I told Almer that partly to confuse him. I am the only survivor of Sharvis's colony."

"Other than Sharvis, himself," Marca said. "Where is he, Take?"

"At this moment? I don't know."

"Where does he live? On the night side? That's where Alodios went and I know that Alodios was looking for him, too."

"Alodios was following an old trail."

"He didn't find Sharvis, after all?" Marca moved to look through the window that faced the night. The red sunlight poured in from the window opposite, throwing dark shadows on the twisted walls of the room. All their faces were tinted by it.

Take seemed to be deep in thought.

"Alodios did find Sharvis eventually," he said.

"Did he give him what he wanted?"

"Sharvis gave him what he thought he wanted, just as he gave me what I thought I wanted once. That is Sharvis's sense of humour, you see. He always gives people what they think they want."

104

"Did you and Alodios want what I wanted?" Marca faced Take. "Did you?"

"More or less, yes. We both wanted immortality, as you did. But Alodios and I did not escape. Luckily, I gather, you saw reason in time."

"So immortality is possible!" Marca exclaimed.

Fastina looked up at Take. "Then why can't Sharvis be found? If the world knew this, the things that have been happening would stop soon enough. If everyone were immortal . . ."

"Sharvis is not idealistic," Take said with a slight, ironic smile. "He would not go to the world with the offer of immortality. If anyone went to him, he would give it to them willingly, but his gift would not be appreciated by many."

"I don't understand," Fastina said. "Why won't you tell us where Sharvis is—so that we can tell others?"

Take laughed humourlessly. The sound was a frightening one and Fastina moved closer to Marca.

"I hate no one sufficiently to send them to Orlando Sharvis and I would advise you, very strongly, never to think of Sharvis again, to assume that he is dead. If I underestimated his power. I would show you things that he had done to warn you away from him, but I know from experience that even these sights are not enough to overcome the fascination Sharvis can exert on the strongest of wills. Listen to my advice—particularly you, Clovis Marca. Stay here where you are safe. You are in love—you can live here together for the rest of your lives. Be as happy as you can be—enjoy each other's love and the life you have." Take's voice was still rich and vibrant, still essentially without expression. He was trying to give his words urgency, trying to use his eyes to emphasise his words, but, strangely, he could not. He spoke emotional words without emotion.

He obviously realised this, for he added: "Consider my words. Take them seriously. Do not become like me."

He began to walk back down the passage, his pace quickening until his movements were a blur of speed.

Marca knew that this time Take could not escape him.

Only he could open the membrane at the entrance to the tower.

He followed the man, shouting after him. The tower and its associations, his conversation with Take, his experiences at the house in Ceylon, all had combined to revive the old, dark thoughts that he had managed to submerge in Fastina's company.

As Marca ran after Take, Fastina ran behind him, calling: "Clovis! Clovis! I'm sure he's right. We'll stay here. Let him go."

Marca caught up with Take at the entrance. The man was trying to force his way through the membrane but it would not yield.

Marca said: "Tell me where Sharvis is, Take! I am my own man—I won't be deceived by him or whatever it is you fear will happen to me. I don't even want what I wanted before when I searched Earth and space for him. But he is a brilliant biologist and physicist. Can't you see that there is a chance he can help the race somehow? He might know of a way to revive the poisoned sperm and ovum, to . . ."

Take leapt forward so quickly that Marca did not realise anything had happened until he felt Take's hand gripping his wrist in a hold that could not be broken.

"Do as I told you," Take said. "Stay here. Forget everything but that girl behind you. Make her happy and let her make you happy. Stay in the tower!"

"And go mad as my father and sister went mad?"

"If it happens, it will be a human madness. Accept it!"

Take hauled Marca forward. Marca tried to resist but Take's strength was incredible. He forced Marca's hand towards the entrance and pushed it flat aganst the barrier. The membrane dropped down. Take dropped Marca's wrist and sped toward the air car.

"You have stocks of food here," he shouted as he took the car upwards. "I will bring you more when I can. I will visit you when I can. I am your friend, Clovis Marca!"

They stood together in the twilight, watching the air car disappear.

106

"We haven't any gravstraps," Marca murmured as Fastina put her hand in his. "And he's taken the car. We couldn't go back if we wanted to—except by walking and the journey is almost impossible as I well know. He has marooned us!"

"He means well, Clovis. Take his advice, please."

"Whether he means well or not, what I said to him I meant, Fastina. I am my own man. I will not be given orders by Take or anyone else."

"You are proud, Clovis. You are proud, after all."

He sighed as they went back into the tower. "I suppose so. Arrogant, Almer said—more arrogant than himself. Does it matter to you, Fastina?"

"Does it to you?" she said.

"It would have done just a little while ago," he told her. "But I'm not sure now."

"Then I don't mind," she smiled. "I don't mind what you are, Clovis. We are together, we are secure, we have each other for all our lives. Isn't that enough for you?"

He drew a deep breath. "You're right," he said. "I can do nothing in the world Almer has created. I should appreciate my exile. Yes, it's enough."

BOOK THREE

CHAPTER ONE

The Tower

But it was not enough. Not eventually.

For over two years they lived together in the tower. They never went out, for there was nowhere to go on that red barren plain. They were in love; that did not change. If anything, their love became fiercer, though their love-making became a shade stranger. They spent the greater part of their time in the huge bed in the deep yellow room. In that bed Clovis's father had been born; in it his wife had conceived and born a daughter; in it father and daughter had coupled and conceived a son. Now the son sported there, but this time there would be no issue.

True to his word, Take visited them from time to time bringing them food and other things they needed. He came fairly regularly, about once every three months. Marca gave up trying to discover from Take where Sharvis was.

Take was reticent, also, about the state of affairs in the daylight world. He mentioned that Andros Almer was now in complete power and that the Brotherhood of Guilt was all but extinguished. On a more personal note he told them that Almer had blamed them not only for the destruction of Narvo's transmitter, but also for Velusi's murder. According to Almer, they had perished by crashing deliberately into the sea.

When not in bed, Marca would read his father's books, or look through tapes of his family history since his ancestors had settled in the twilight region. There was a strong resemblance between all the men and many of the women towards the end. Valta Marca and his daughter Betild might have been twins as far as appearance was concerned, and for that matter Clovis Marca could have been a twin to either. They all had the same tall, delicate-boned bodies, the large eyes and heavy brows and broad cheekbones. Marca began to identify with them again and think that he was a fool to have left the tower for the daylight region and that there was only one good thing that had resulted from that boyhood decision—Fastina.

He would wander back through the twisting, crystal corridors that were bathed in dim, shifting light, and seek her out.

Their need for each other was almost always so strong that they could not bear to be apart for more than an hour at a time.

Sometimes they quarrelled, but not often and never for long. Sometimes, more frequently, they would lie side by side hating each other with such an intensity that they would have to make love or kill the other person, and the love-making then was brutal and selfish.

Marca devised a trap for Take. It was modelled on something his father had made for slaughtering animals. There was no game in this part of the twilight region, so it had never been used. It was one of many such useless inventions of his father, who had turned his attention to such things after Betild's death.

It was a couch now. It had been a bench. The couch was broad, but could curl up on itself rather like a Venus flytrap and crush or stifle whatever lay in it. It would not be strong enough to kill a man like Take, but it would hold him and give Marca a chance to question him.

Marca's desire to question Take was no longer based on any particular wish to act on the information he might get; he had lost sight of that. His single obsession now was somehow to get his jailer at a disadvantage—get him in his power if only for a short time.

The couch could be controlled by a little device that Marca kept in his pocket when dressed.

He had tried to get Take to sit on the couch the last time the man had visited them, but Take had not stayed long enough.

Fastina did not know about the couch. He kept it in his father's room, where he kept the books and tapes.

Time passed, though they had no record of its passing and there were no signs outside until the rains came.

The rains came infrequently to this part of the world, but when they came it was for days at a time. They welcomed the change in the climate and would sit by the windows watching the water mingle with the dust and turn it to mud. It fell without pause in a great, pounding sheet.

It was during this rainfall that the vigilante found the tower.

CHAPTER TWO

The Pursuit

The vigilante landed his small, one-man air car close to the entrance of the tower. The rain fell on the force bubble protecting him and washed over it.

They watched from a small window as the man drew his cloak about him, switched off his force screen and dashed for the entrance.

"What shall we do?" Fastina said to Marca who was thoughtfully rubbing his lips with his fingers.

Marca had suddenly thought of a new plan.

"We must let him in," he told her, getting up and making for the entrance. "Perhaps Almer found a record of this place as my family home and sent him to investigate."

"We can't let him in. He's armed. He might kill us."

"An assassin would have come more cautiously. I'll let him in." He paused for a moment. "You stay out of sight, Fastina. I'll take him to my father's room. If you think I'm in trouble, you'll be able to help better if he doesn't know you're here."

She nodded mutely, her large eyes full of anxiety.

Marca went along the passage and saw the outline of the vigilante as the man tried to push his way through the protecting membrane.

Marca stared through at the black-masked, hooded face. The mask was edged with light blue. The man was not, after all, Almer himself.

The vigilante gesticulated, spreading his hands, trying to show that he came in peace.

Marca put his palm against the membrane and it folded down to the floor.

The vigilante recovered himself and swaggered through, one gloved hand on his sword-hilt. There was another weapon at his belt. Marca recognised it as a gun of some kind.

There was a damp, musty smell from the vigilante's cloak as he entered and watched as the membrane shimmered back into place.

"A peculiar sort of device," the stranger said, indicating the membrane. "I've seen nothing like it before."

Marca said, with a trace of humour, "It was an invention of my father's. Only members of my family can make it open or close. Since I'm the last surviving member of my family, you would do well to remember that only my *living* hand can open it and let you out."

The stranger shrugged.

"I haven't come to offer you any harm, Clovis Marca. On the contrary, I have come . . ."

"Tell me in my study," Marca said. He led the way up the winding, sloping crystal passage until they reached his father's room.

"A strange, bizarre sort of place," the stranger said as Marca poured him a drink. He sat on the couch, lounging back and raising a hand to refuse the drink. "No thanks—old habit—never trust an offer of food or drink in my job."

Marca drank the wine himself. "What is your job?"

"I am Security Scout 008, especially commissioned to find you by our leader himself."

"Almer knew where I was? How long has he known?"

"Our leader only suspected you could be here. Since you did not seem to offer him much immediate harm, he did not bother to check his suspicion. He has more important things on his mind."

"What kind of things? What has been happening back there?"

"I'm coming to that, Clovis Marca. The Control has succeeded in establishing order and peace throughout the daylight world. It is a tribute to Chief Control, our leader, that the old Brotherhood of Guilt has been virtually stamped out or driven underground and now offers no threat to the security of the people. The birth struggles, perhaps, were what you witnessed and, looking back, we can see that these might well have horrified you . . ."

Marca interrupted suspiciously. "The Control? Is this the term you now use to describe the vigilantes?"

"It is. Having established the Rule of Law, we decided the old term was no longer functional." The man's pale lips smiled. "We were forced to do certain things at the beginning, but they enabled us to bring peace and security to a disordered society. You would not recognise it now, Clovis Marca . . ."

"I'm sure I wouldn't." The terms and phrasing were familiar to Marca from his reading. He could imagine the repression that must now exist throughout the daylight world.

"Instead of the old, hard to administer, system of living, we now have all houses grouped in strictly-defined areas. This enables us to deal with the needs of the people with greater efficiency and also makes it more difficult for violent elements to threaten . . ."

"Don't go on," Marca told him. "Just explain why you're here."

The security scout looked down at his hands and cleared his throat gently. "Your old friend needs your help," he said.

"My old friend? You mean Almer?" Marca laughed.

"I am told to say that he realises he did you harm in the past, but that he thinks you will now recognise the difficulty he was in, establishing order in the world. Some people have to suffer in order that the majority . . ."

"He killed my closest friend," Marca said. "He killed Brand Calax, too. He killed people working on Velusi's transmitter—idealistic, innocent people. He murdered scores . . ."

"Hundreds," said the scout, with a touch of pride. "But it was necessary for the common good."

113

"And now he has mellowed, has he?" Marca said sardonically. "He only kills a few every so often. Soon only Andros Almer will be left . . ."

"He appreciates the anger you must feel," the scout continued imperturbably. "But he thinks your sense of duty—always marked in the past—will make you understand that now he needs your help in order to control the ordered society he has created . . ."

"He has created nothing but ignorance and misery. The race will peter out of existence in fear and despair. That is all he has done for the world."

"It is a matter of opinion. Please let me finish, Clovis Marca."

"Very well."

"Chief Control has discovered recalcitrant elements amongst his upper echelon officers . . ."

"Only to be expected. He knew this would happen, surely?"

". . . and these officers have managed to get a great deal of support in the more naïve sections of the community. They have used your name . . ."

"My name?"

". . . your name to convince the people that they are guided only by idealism and wish to return the world to what they call the paradise it was before our leader restored order. They tell the people that you have returned and are secretly in charge of this splinter-group."

"So they plan to overthrow Almer and set themselves up in his place—and continue in the same way as Almer."

"They have not our leader's principles and strength of mind. Society will collapse as they war among themselves . . ."

"I know the pattern. What does Almer want of me?"

"He offers you joint command with him as Chief Control if you will return and give your support to him."

Marca did not reply immediately. He had the feeling that the story was just a little too glib. If Almer had already blackened his name as Velusi's murderer, why did that name now carry weight amongst the ordinary people? He was almost certain that this was a trap of Almer's to get him out of his tower and into a position where he could be killed easily. He must still represent a threat to Almer—and Almer must still want Fastina Cahmin.

"So Almer needs my help," he smiled. "I can't believe that. What are you to do if I refuse?"

"Take your message back to our leader."

"And what then?"

"He has another plan—to tell the people where you are hiding and then launch a heavily publicised attack on this place and destroy you—thus checking his officers' plans. You would do better to accept this offer. If you accept he will send a carriage to collect you."

"This tower is invulnerable. He would waste his time attacking it."

"That's as may be—but we are developing strong weapons nowadays. You are not as secure as you think."

"You said Almer was not sure I was here?"

"I did." The scout placed a hand on the butt of his gun. "I have a commission to try here and then try the other towers in the region. If I do not return in a month or so he will check to see what has happened to me."

"A month?"

The scout tightened his grip on the gun butt, looking into Marca's eyes, obviously guessing why Marca was asking these questions."

"And if I am offered violence, Clovis Marca, I am instructed to kill you."

"You forget that you cannot get out of here unless I am alive."

The man hesitated, glancing instinctively towards the door.

Marca reached into his pocket and pressed the single stud on the little device he had there.

The sides of the couch curled in on the scout well before he could drag the gun from its holster. Slowly, they began to squeeze in on the frightened man.

The couch had been designed to have enough force to hold, but not harm, a man of outstanding strength like Take.

The black-masked scout had only ordinary strength.

The couch began to crush him and he began to scream.

Marca turned away. This was the first creature he had ever knowingly killed.

He covered his ears as the man's screams changed to a panting gurgle and bones crunched as the couch slowly squeezed him to death.

Marca shuddered. Tears ran down his face, but he knew he could not stop what he was doing. The man was as good as dead already.

In a short while the man stopped making any noise at all.

Marca looked back at the couch. It was folded neatly in on itself.

A little blood seeped out of it, but that was the only sign of what had happened.

Then he looked towards the entrance of the room and saw Fastina leaning there, her face covered by her hands. She must have heard the screams and come to the room, thinking Marca was in trouble. She must have seen the scout's death.

Marca crossed the room and guided her out of it, up the sloping, winding passage to the yellow room. He made her lie down on the disordered bed. He went to the window and, for the first time since he had been there, opened it.

The rain swept in to the room, and the cold air came with it. The water washed over the floor and Marca stood by the window, the rain beating at his face, beating at his hands and body, soaking his clothing.

Fastina began to sob from where she lay with her face buried in the bedclothes, but Marca did not hear her, and eventually Fastina fell asleep while Marca continued to stand stock still by the window, letting the rain lash his face.

After a long while, he turned, closed the window, covered Fastina with dry blankets from a cupboard, and went to dispose of the couch and what it contained.

The couch went into the incinerator easily enough. The last corpse Marca had put in it had been his father's.

He wrapped a heavy cloak about him and went to the

entrance of the tower, opening it and slopping through the thin, red mud to the air car. He reached into it and activated its controls so that it drifted just above the ground. Then he began to drag it towards the tower.

The rain made it difficult to see, and twice he slipped in the mud, but eventually he got the air car into the tower and began guiding it through the passages to his father's room where he put it where the couch had been and covered it with a large cloth.

Now he was ready for Take's next visit. He went to bed.

Take came a week later, with his air car full of provisions.

The rain had stopped and the mud had hardened to earth which would soon become dust again. It was already cracking as Take, his shadow long and black behind him, hauled the sack of foodstuffs from the landed air car and stumbled towards the tower.

Marca greeted him with apparent cheerfulness. Fastina was still in bed, where she had been since Marca had murdered the scout. She had recovered a little and evidently did not blame him for what he had done, since she believed the scout had tried to kill Marca, but she had not been willing to talk much and this had suited him as he had waited impatiently for Take's arrival.

Take noticed the difference in Marca's manner as he entered the tower. "You seem in better spirits," he said.

Together they dragged the provisions into the nearest room and Take sat down in one of the grotesque chairs.

"I don't feel too badly, for a prisoner," Marca replied. "Perhaps the rain washed my depression away. Have you seen Orlando Sharvis recently?"

"Not recently—only the effects of his work. You are well off here, my friend."

"I wish you would let me decide that," Marca replied equably.

"How is Fastina Cahmin?"

"In bed. She's sleeping."

"Sleeping? She's lucky. Do you sleep often?"

It was a strange question. "Frequently," smiled Marca.

He sat down opposite Take. "Why do you ask?"

"I envy you, that's all." Take's head began to sink forward in the familiar, lopsided way, and he straightened it slowly. It was almost as if his neck were broken, Marca thought.

"You don't sleep well, Mr. Take?"

"I don't sleep at all, Clovis Marca. You are a very lucky man. I wish I were the 'prisoner' and someone else the 'jailer', as you put it . . ."

"I would be the first to agree," Marca smiled. "Can I offer you something to eat? A drink?"

"No. Is there anything you particularly want me to bring on my next visit?"

"Nothing."

"Then I will get back." Take raised himself to his feet.

Marca escorted him to the door and opened it for Take. He did not close it again, but said hurriedly, "I think I heard Fastina call. Goodbye, Mr. Take."

"Goodbye," Take began to trudge towards the golden air car he was still using.

Marca ran rapidly through the corridors to his father's room, tore off the coverings from the small one-man air car and jumped into it.

At a crazy speed, he drove it through the passages, twisting down and down until he reached the entrance. He slowed the car. There was a glint of gold in the dark sky.

The air car was equipped with a fixing device. Marca adjusted his speed, homed the air car on the one above, and began to climb into the air, leaving the tower, and Fastina, behind him.

This had been his reason for murdering the scout. Now he could follow Take to wherever the man came from.

He suspected that Take would lead him to Orlando Sharvis.

CHAPTER THREE

The Cage

Take's air car was heading deeper and deeper into the night.

Marca had suspected that it would, which was partly why he had not relied on keeping the golden car in sight but had made sure his own car's instruments would follow it. As the light got fainter, the shadows lengthened until they merged into a general darkness and the air became cold.

The car, built only to be used in the daylight and twilight, had no heater and Marca huddled in his cloak wishing he had brought more clothing.

At last it became pitch black and Marca could see nothing of the land below and above him were only massive clouds and the occasional stars. The moon had been hurled down into the sea by the space-dwellers when they had brought the Earth to a gradual stop. It now lay in the North Pacific somewhere, with much of its bulk below the surface.

The air became damper and even colder. Unable to see his instruments, Marca had no clear idea where he was now, although, judging by the air, he was probably over one of the many ice fields that covered both land and sea on the nightside of Earth.

As he travelled his perceptions became dulled and his contact with reality so tenuous that it did not occur to him to protect himself by means of the car's force-screen.

Much later, when his body was numb with cold and he

was half-certain he was going to die, the air car began to fall in a gradual dive.

Looking over the side of the craft, he just made out the glint of ice, reflecting the sparse starlight, and ahead was a dark outline that seemed to be a great mountain range, though it was peculiarly rounded. The air car was heading straight for this.

Marca wondered if Take had led him into a trap and if he was going to crash into the side of the curved mountain that protruded from the ice-flats. The air car sped nearer. It was only then that Marca switched on his force-screen to help cushion the impact he anticipated.

No impact came. Instead the car reached the cliff and kept going. It had entered a great cave in the face of the cliff.

The air car continued to sweep downward through the utter darkness of the gigantic tunnel and Marca's air became foul in time so that he was forced to switch off the force-screen.

To Marca's relief, it was much warmer in the tunnel.

Deeper and deeper down the tunnel went the air car, banking occasionally to take turns, until a faint light could be seen ahead.

As the light increased, Marca could see the walls of the tunnel, far away on both sides of him. The tunnel was obviously artificial and could take a large spaceship.

The air car began to slow as it reached the source of light and eventually stopped altogether, moving into the side of the tunnel. There, in a niche, Marca saw the golden air car that had once belonged to Fastina. Take seemed to have hidden it there.

Running his hand over the rock, Marca gradually realised where he was.

He was in the moon itself, now far below the surface of the Pacific.

He searched through the little air car until he found a gravstrap in a locker. He fitted it under his arms and left the air car, drifting cautiously forward towards the blaze of light ahead.

The light hurt his eyes for a while, as the tunnel opened

120

out into a vast, artificial cavern.

Shielding his eyes, Marca looked upwards into the 'sky' and saw the source of both the heat and the light. It was a globe of energy, pulsating slightly: a man-made sun.

Below was a rolling landscape of what appeared to be scarlet and black moss that was relieved in the distance by slim, jagged crags of brown rock. The 'sky' itself was a lurid orange colour, fading to pink near the horizon.

It was a world of rudimentary and primordial colours, like a planet half-created and then abandoned. But this place had been created by a man—or at least some intelligent agency.

Marca guessed who the man had been. He thought he had found where Orlando Sharvis lived.

How long had it taken to hollow out the moon and make this tiny world within it? Why had Sharvis made the world in the first place?

Marca began to feel afraid. He could see nothing of Take, and the rest of the place seemed deserted. Ahead of him now was a tall mass of rock, a plateau rising suddenly out of the scarlet and black moss surrounding it.

Through the warm, utterly still air, Marca drifted along on his gravstrap, heading towards the bluff.

As he rose above the level of the cliff top, the first thing he saw was the metal. In the distance it looked like a great, static mobile, only momentarily at rest. Multi-angled surfaces flashed and glared.

The thing lay in a depression on the plateau, ringed by rocks that all leaned inwards so that the object seemed to lie in the gullet of some sharp-toothed beast. The rocks were long, black fangs, casting a network of shadows into the depression. Sometimes the individual surfaces would merge as he turned his head, and then the whole would combine—a blaze of bright metal—and as suddenly disintegrate again.

Only as he got closer did Marca realise that this was a settlement of some kind: a peculiar shanty-town with shacks of gold, silver, ruby, emerald and diamond, built from sheets of harder-than-steel plastic and metal. They all seemed to lean against one another for support; were placed at random, forming a cluttered jungle of artificial materials on the barren rock.

Soon Marca could make out individual buildings. All were single storeyed. There too were patches of cultivated land, small, deep reservoirs, featureless cabinets of machinery, and thin cables.

There seemed to have been no design to this strange village. It appeared to have grown little by little and it was quite plain that whoever lived there existed in conditions far more primitive than anyone else on the planet. Why? Surely they had a choice? They did not need to live in an artificial world, artificially maintained.

Marca dropped to the ground, within the circle of black rocks but beyond the limits of the village.

Now he could see one or two figures moving slowly between the shanties.

From the ground, the place did not look quite so makeshift, though it was also evident that the shanties were not made of prefabricated parts but constructed from the plates of spaceships and other large machines.

Marca walked cautiously forward.

And then a tall old man, with curling white hair, a cream-coloured cloak, yellow tights and a huge box strapped to his naked chest, appeared from behind the nearest building and greeted him.

"Stranger, you are welcome," he said gravely, dropping his chin to his chest and staring hard at Marca. "You enter a holy place, the Seat of the Centre, Influencer of the Spheres—come, pilgrim!" With a great show of dignity he swept his arm to indicate a low, narrow doorway.

Marca did not move. He recognised the jargon. The man was a member of the new Deistic Church of the Zodiac, a cult that had flourished before the raid but which had died out after it.

"Who are you?" he said. "How long have you been here?"

"I have no name. I am the guardian of the Seat of the Centre and I have been here for eternity."

The man was mad.

"What's that box fixed to your chest?" Marca peered at it. Wires seemed to leave the box and enter the man's body. "What is it?"

"Box? There is no 'box'!". The demented old man bent and disappeared into the doorway.

Marca continued to move through the village. From the shanties he heard stirrings and soft voices, low moans and whines that were either human or mechanical, heard a scraping noise once or twice, but saw no one until he entered a small clearing.

There, to one side, in the shade of a building, sat a man. Marca went up to him. The man stared out at him but his eyes did not move as Marca knelt beside him.

"Can you tell me what this place is?" Marca asked.

"Heaven," said the man tonelessly, without looking at Marca. He began to laugh in a dry, hopeless voice. Marca straightened up.

Further on he saw something that appeared at first to be nothing but a tangle of coils and thin cables, a dark, static web standing nearly two meters high and some sixty centimetres in diameter, of a dull, red colour with threads of blue, gold and silver closer to its centre. As he got closer Marca saw the outlines of a human figure inside the web. A clear, pleasant voice came from it.

"Good morning, newcomer. I saw you approaching across the fields. What a warm day it is."

"Fields?" Marca said. "There are no fields. You mean the moss?"

The voice chuckled. "You must have been in a daze. You have only just left them. You came past the farm and walked along the lane and came through the gate there and now you are here. I like visitors."

Marca began to realise that the man was living an illusion, just as the other old man he had first met. Was this the function of the village? Did people come here to have their illusions made into some sort of reality? He recognised the basic design of the machine in which the man sat. It was one of many invented in an effort to defeat the effects of the space ache. Every function of a man's mind and body was controlled by the machine which completely simulated an Earthly environment for him. The thing had worked quite well, except it left a man all but useless for anything but piloting a space-ship and, it was discovered later, it spread a peculiar kind of cancer through the spinal fluid and the resulting death was worse than the space ache. Also once the thing was connected, it had to stay connected, for disconnection generally resulted in an acute psychic shock that brought death instantly.

The cage of metal moved jerkily forward. From inside it an emaciated hand reached out and touched Marca's arm. "You," said the clear voice. "You. You. You." It paused. "Me," it said at length. Then the encaged figure turned and went back to its original position.

Marca moved on. The man he had questioned had called the place heaven, but it seemed more like hell. This was like somewhere that might have existed in pre-raid days. The village seemed populated only by the insane.

He knocked on the wall of the nearest shack. He called "Is anyone in?" He bent his head and entered the room. The smell was terrible. Inside the room, on a big, square mattress, a young man sat up suddenly. Beside him lay a young woman.

But were they young? Looking closer, Marca could see that they had the appearance of old people whose flesh had somehow been artificially padded and whose skin had been worked to remove all signs of age.

"Get out!" said the man.

Outside, Marca sighed and looked around him. He began to feel that it would be wiser to leave the village and return to his air car and then make his way back to the tower and Fastina.

Why had these people come here? Why had they subjected themselves to such a dreadful existence?

He found another man. This one's skull was open to reveal his brain. Electrodes poked out of it and were fixed to a box on his back. The brain was protected by some kind of force screen. The man himself looked quite normal.

"Why are you here?" Marca asked him.

The man's smile was melancholy. "Because I wanted to be."

"Did Orlando Sharvis do this to you?"

"Yes."

"As punishment?"

The man's smile broadened. "Of course not. I asked him to do it. Do you realise that I am probably the most intelligent man in the world thanks to all this?" He pointed a thumb at the box on his back. Then an expression of fear came over his face.

"You mustn't delay me. I must hurry."

"Why?"

"The power-pack uses an enormous amount of energy. It must be recharged every twenty minutes, or I die." The man stumbled away between the shanties.

"Sharvis giveth and Sharvis taketh away," said a maliciously amused voice behind Marca. Marca did not recognise the quotation, but he recognised the face as he turned.

The man was pale-faced and thin-lipped and he had bitter eyes. He was dressed in a loose black toga and on his hands were a great many rings. The jewels in the rings were Ganymedian dream-gems. By concentrating on them, one could rapidly hypnotise oneself.

The man's name was Philas Damiago who had once had the reputation of being the world's last murderer, though his victim had been revived in time and lived to die of old age. Damiago had disappeared a hundred and fifty years before, but his face was familiar to Marca from the history tapes. Marca thought ironically that Damiago would now be merely one among many if he returned to the daylight.

"Philas Damiago?"

"I am, indeed. Do you recognise the origin of the quotation?"

"I'm afraid not."

"You are not a literary man?"

"I think I'm well-read, but . . ."

"It comes from the old Christian Bible—the English

125

translation. I used to read that a lot, as well as more or less contemporary works—Shakespeare, Milton, Tolstoy, Hëdsen. You know them?"

"I know of them. I have read a little of them all, I think."

"I was a scholar, you know. Ancient literature was my speciality. I became too absorbed in it, I suppose . . ."

"You murdered your brother . . ."

"Exactly. All that blood and death, my friend. It went to my head."

"You've been here ever since?"

Damiago shook his head. "No. Originally I went to the twilight region. I was there for some time. Then I came here."

"Looking for Orlando Sharvis, I suppose."

"Yes. As these others had done before me—and since."

"You do not seem as affected as they are."

Damiago smiled. "Not externally."

"What did you want from Sharvis?"

"Time. I wanted time to study every work of literature that had ever been written and time in which to write my history of literature."

"Sharvis gave you time?"

"Oh, yes. He operated on me. I can now live for at least another five hundred years."

"Surely that is enough time to do what you want to do."

"Certainly." Damiago's mouth moved as if to add something.

"Then what's the trouble?" Marca felt impatient. He wanted to find Take.

"The operation affected my brain—my eyes. I am word blind."

Marca felt sorry for Damiago. "In the circumstances you have kept remarkably sane. You must be very strong minded, Damiago."

Damiago shrugged. "I have ways of staying sane. I have my work—new work. Would you like to see it?"

Damiago strode towards a hut and entered it. Marca followed him. The place was well lit and bigger than he expected. In the centre, on a plinth, surrounded by tools and furniture, stood a great half-finished sculpture. It was a crude thing, yet powerful. The whole thing was constructed from human bones.

Marca changed his opinion of Damiago. The man was only apparently sane.

"Do you hunt for your materials . . . ?" Marca asked harshly, trying to humour the man.

"Oh, no. They come to me eventually. I'm the most valuable member of the community, really. They want to die—I need their bones. Perhaps, in time, you, too, will come to me?"

"I don't think so."

"You never know. You are looking for Orlando Sharvis, are you not? You will not go away, having seen what will happen to you?"

"I might well go away."

"Sensible." Damiago sat on the edge of the plinth. "Go away, then. Goodbye."

"First I want to find out more about this place. I think Alodios, the artist, came here. And a man called Take . . ."

"You're hesitating already. I advised Alodios against going to see Orlando Sharvis, and I advise you, likewise. But it will do no good."

"Does Sharvis resent visitors?"

"On the contrary, he welcomes them. He will welcome you, particularly when you tell him what you want. You do want something from him, of course?"

"I suppose so. But I did not really come to see Sharvis. I'm not even sure now why I came at all. But now I'm here, I'd like to see Alodios, at least. I knew him well . . ."

"If you did, then don't go to see him."

"Where is he?"

Damiago spread his hands and then pointed. "He lives about a hundred kilometres to the right over there. You'll see a cluster of high rocks. Alodios lives there. Sharvis lives in the mountains to the north-east of there—you will see the mountains from the cliff. His laboratories extend throughout the mountains. You will see a tall shaft of polished stone. That will show you where the entrance to the laboratories lies."

"I told you—I didn't think I wanted to see Sharvis now."

Damiago nodded. "If you say so."

Clovis Marca stood on the edge of the cliff beneath the artificial sun. Next to him was a high-backed chair in which sat a silent man.

For the second time, Marca said politely: "Alodios? Am I disturbing you?" But the seated figure did not reply or move.

Nervously, Marca stepped closer.

"Alodios. It is Clovis Marca."

He moved around the chair. He was careful where he put his feet for he was very close to the edge. It was a long, sheer drop to the red and black moss below.

Alodios continued to stare fixedly outwards. The sun in his eyes did not seem to bother him. Marca wondered if he were dead.

"Alodios?"

There was great character written in the old man's face and hands, in the very shape of his body. He was a big man, with great hard muscles, a broad chest and huge arms and hands. His head was of similar proportions, strong and massive, with thick dark hair framing it. Heavy black eyebrows bristled on his jutting brow, heavily lidded eyes were half-closed, but the black eyes could be seen. The nose was acquiline and the mouth seemed the mouth of a bird of prey, also. The full lips were turned downwards in a way that was at once cruel, sensitive and sardonic. But it was all frozen, as if Alodios were a living statue. Only the eyes lived. Suddenly, they looked at him.

In his horror Marca almost lost his footing on the cliff. There was absolute torment in the eyes. From that frozen face they stared out at him, without self-pity, without any true intelligence. It was as if some mute, uncomprehending beast were trapped in the skull, for it was not the look of a man at all. It was the look of a tortured animal.

Alodios plainly did not think now. He felt, only. Sense

128

was gone, leaving only sensibility. Marca could not bear to look into the eyes for long. He turned away.

Alodios had been a genius. His intellect and sensitivity, his creative powers, had been unmatched in history. He had created great novels—combinations of poetry, prose, pictures, sculpture, music and acted drama that had reached the peak of artistic expression. Now it was as if something had destroyed the intelligence but left the sensitive core unsullied. He was still receptive, still aware—but with no mind to rationalise the impressions.

Marca thought that there could be no worse experience than this. For Alodios's sake, he began to push the chair towards the very edge of the cliff. Alodios would crash to the bottom and die.

A voice came from behind him, then. "I doubt if that will do any good, Clovis Marca." It was Take's rich voice.

Marca turned. Take stood there with his head on one side, dressed in his dark clothes, with his white hands clasped before him.

"Why won't it do any good?"

"He has what you wanted."

"This? This isn't what I wanted!"

"He has immortality. Alodios went to Orlando Sharvis and Orlando Sharvis played a joke on him. Alodios found immortality, but he lost the sense of passing time."

"A *joke*?" Marca could hardly speak. "Alodios was the greatest . . ."

"Yes. Sharvis knew what he was. That, you see, was the joke."

After a moment, Marca said: "Isn't there any way of killing Alodios?"

"I think you would find him invulnerable, as I am."

"You are immortal, Mr. Take? I thought so."

Take laughed flatly. "I am immortal. I am a superman. My reflexes are ten times faster, my strength ten times greater, my reasoning powers ten times better than they were. I cannot be destroyed—I cannot destroy myself, even! Only Sharvis, who made me, can destroy me. And he refuses. I was his first immortal. I was a soldier, originally, who escaped with him after the Last Wars. I was his chief lieutenant when he had gathered his Titan expedition together. By that time he had experimented on myself and two others. They had died, but I had survived. I wanted immortality at the time. It may sound strange, but I was prepared to risk dying for it. We went to Titan after he had operated on himself in the same way. It was because of these operations that we were able to survive Titan."

"The others?"

"In spite of more and more experiments on their bodies, they died one by one. Sharvis and I returned to Earth —to the night side and the moon."

"How did you create this world?"

"We had begun work on it before we left. This was where the Titan ship was built. He has machines—they can do anything. He gets his raw materials either from the moon itself, or else from the sea-beds."

"And you found immortality unbearable. Why was that?"

"He gave me immortality, but took my life."

" 'Sharvis giveth and Sharvis taketh away'," murmured Marca. "That's what Damiago said. You know Damiago?"

"I know them all. It is I who look after them. Sharvis does not."

Marca looked towards the mountains far away. "That's where Sharvis has his laboratories, Damiago said. Surely, Take, he has the means to do anything—to revive our diseased cells—make the world well again . . . If I paid Sharvis a visit . . ."

Take lunged forward, arms outstretched, and, before Marca realised it, the man had hurled him over the cliff.

Marca, as he fell, almost welcomed the fact that he was going to die. In killing him, Take had absolved him from all responsibility. Then, automatically, he had squeezed his gravstrap and began to float gently downward. More pressure on the strap and he was rising again.

Take was waiting for him, arms folded.

"As you see, Clovis Marca, I am in earnest. I would kill you rather than let you go to Sharvis. You do not under-

130

tand the fascination that he can exert."

Marca sank back to the ground. Nearby he saw a piece
f loose rock. He stooped and picked it up.

"The only point you have made, Take, is to prove your-
elf as irrational as anyone. How do I know that your
udgment of Sharvis is the correct one? You hate him be-
ause he gave you something you wanted. Is he to blame
or that?"

"You see," Take said. "Your mind is already twisting.
f you persist, if you will not return to the tower with me,
must kill you. It will be an act of mercy."

"I still wish to decide for myself."

"I will not let you."

Marca flung the jagged rock at Take.

Take reached out and caught it. Then he moved to-
vards Marca, his arm raised.

Marca pressed his gravstrap and began to rise into the
ir, but Take seized his ankle and hauled him to the
round. He swung his rock and smashed it down on Mar-
a's head. Marca felt nothing, but he knew he was dead.

CHAPTER FOUR

The Resurrection

In his last moment of life, Clovis Marca had realised how much he wanted to live and had at the same time been reconciled to the fact that he was dead; yet now he was conscious again and full of infinite relief.

He opened his eyes and saw nothing but a milky whiteness. He became frightened suddenly and shut his eyes tightly. Was he dead, after all? He seemed to be drifting weightlessly, unable to feel the presence of his own body.

It seemed that he remained with his eyes shut for hours before he opened them again, curiosity overcoming his fear.

Now in front of him something crystalline winked and shimmered. Beyond the crystal a shape moved, but he could not define what it was. He turned his head and saw more crystal, with dim outlines behind it. He tried to move a leg, but could feel nothing. Something happened, however. His body began to turn slowly and he could see that he was completely surrounded by the crystal. Attached to his mouth was a muzzle and leading away from it were several slender tubes which seemed imbedded in the crystal. He could look down and see the rest of his body.

With some difficulty he stretched out his hand and touched the irregular surface of the crystal. It tingled and made him feel less intangible. He tried to make some sound with his mouth. The muzzle stopped him from speaking, but he managed a muffled murmur. The awareness that at least he retained his senses of sight touch and hearing reassured him.

He closed his eyes again and lifted his hand to his head, but could feel nothing.

Far away, a voice said softly, "Ah, good. You will be out of there soon, now."

Then Marca fell asleep.

He woke up and he was lying on a couch in a small, featureless room. It was warm and he felt very comfortable. He looked around, but could not see a door in the room. He looked up. There were indications that the room's entrance was in the roof directly above the couch. He could make out fine indentations forming a square.

He swung himself off the couch. He felt very fit and relaxed, but there was the slight feeling of being watched. Perhaps the walls of his room could be seen through from the other side.

He saw that he was dressed in a one-piece garment of soft, blue material.

He touched his head. It had been partly shaven where Take's rock had struck it and there was an indication of an old, healed scar, but nothing more.

He had been dead and someone had revived him. Had this been a second warning from Take? His brain must have been damaged, he was sure, and only a few surgeons in the world were capable of the operation necessary to revive a man with a bad head injury of that kind.

Orlando Sharvis? It could only have been the mysterious immortal.

A voice whispered and hissed through the room. At first it sounded like a wind sighing through trees, but then Marca recognised words.

"Yes, Clovis Marca. It is Sharvis who has saved you. Sit back—sleep—and soon, I assure you, Sharvis will be at your service . . ."

Marca returned to the couch, aware, but somehow not surprised, that Sharvis could read his thoughts. He lay down and slept again.

The next time he awoke he was still on the couch but it was rising towards the ceiling and the ceiling was opening upward to let him pass. He entered a far larger room, adorned with fluorescent walls of a constantly changing variety of colours. The walls moved like flames and dimly lighted the room.

"Forgive the rather gloomy appearance," said a voice only slightly less sibilant than the one he had first heard, "but I find it hard to bear too much direct light these days. As you guessed, I am Orlando Sharvis. You have been seeking me a long time. I gather, then you gave up, but now you are here. Your unconscious mind was taking you towards me all the time. You realise that now, of course."

"Of course," Marca agreed.

"Then it is a mutual pleasure that we are able to meet at last. As I said, I am at your service . . ."

Marca turned and looked up at Orlando Sharvis.

He had expected to see a man, but he saw a monster; albeit a beautiful monster.

Orlando Sharvis's head resembled a snake's. He had a long, tapering face of mottled red and pink. He had faceted eyes like a fly, a flat, well-shaped nose and a shrunken, toothless mouth.

His body was not at all snake-like. It was almost square and very heavy. His legs were short and firm. His arms and hands, when he moved them, seemed sinuously boneless.

Marca's first impression, however, was one of height, for Orlando Sharvis was nearly ten feet tall.

Bizarre as he was, there was something attractive about him; something, as Take had said, completely fascinating. He could not always have looked like this . . .

"You are right," whispered Sharvis, "my body is the result of extended experiments over a great many years. I have made alterations not merely for convenience, but also to satisfy my own aesthetic tastes and curiosity."

Sharvis was casually reading his mind.

"Another of my experiments that succeeded quite well," Sharvis told him. "Although I must admit that my ability is not perfect. Your mind is, in fact, something of a mystery to me—it harbours so many paradoxical thoughts . . ."

"How did you find me?" Marca asked. His speech was slightly slurred.

134

"A minor invention of mine to bring me information from not only everywhere in the moon, but everywhere in the world. It is a device a little larger than a poppy seed. Call it a micro-eye. I use many thousands of them. I saw what the ungrateful Take did to you and I sent one of my machines to pick you up and bring you here."

"How long have I been here?"

"About a month, I'm afraid. The initial operation failed. I nearly lost you. You need not worry, incidentally, that I have tampered with your mind or body in any way. If you find you are a little numb or that speaking is at first difficult, be assured that the effects will soon disappear. I pride myself that I have done a perfect repair. Your hair growth has been accelerated as you will discover."

Marca touched the top of his head. The bald part of his scalp was now covered in hair again.

"How do you feel generally?" Sharvis asked.

"Very well." But now memories were returning—the colony outside, Alodios, what Take had told him about Sharvis . . .

"Again, I must be candid," Sharvis said. "Perhaps I will lose your trust, but I must tell you the truth. I did perform an operation on your artist friend, although I warned him of the consequences. Yet he still insisted. Every one of those others you saw were also warned that there would probably be side effects to their operations—and every one begged me to continue." The tiny mouth smiled. "I am an equable soul, Clovis Marca. I only do for people what they ask. I use no coercion. If you are thinking of my Last Wars days, please realise that I was young and headstrong then. I knew no humility. Now I know much. The Titan expedition and its failure taught me that."

"You could give me immortality, then?"

"If you wanted it."

"And what's the price?"

Sharvis laughed softly. "Price? Not your 'soul', if that's what you mean—and I see you have some such thought in your mind. You mean your individuality—something like that? I assure you it would remain intact. I am here only to serve you, as I said; to give you your heart's desire."

"Take seemed to think you were guided more by malice than by idealism . . ."

"Take and I have known each other too long for me to regard him with complete objectivity, and the same is true of him. Perhaps we hate each other—but it is an old, sentimental hatred, you understand. I gave Take his freedom. I gave him immortality. Are those the actions of a malicious man?"

Sharvis had a power that was almost hypnotic. Marca found himself unable to think with anything like his old clarity. It was probably the after-effects of the operation.

"You have been guilty of many crimes in the past . . ." Marca began heavily.

"Crimes? No. I serve no abstract Good or Evil. I have no time for mysticism. I am entirely neutral—a scientist. When called upon, I do only what is asked of me. It is the truth."

Marca frowned. "But good and evil are not abstract—ethics are necessary, there are fundamental things which . . ."

"I have no ethic other than my will to serve. Do you believe me?"

"Yes, I believe that."

"Well, then?"

"I see your point of view . . ."

"Good. I am not pressing you to accept any gift of mine, Clovis Marca. I have revived you, you are well, you may leave here whenever you wish . . ."

Marca said uncertainly: "Could I possibly stay for a while—to make up my mind?"

"You are free to go wherever you like in my laboratories. You are my guest."

"And if I decided to ask you for immortality . . . ?"

Orlando Sharvis raised a sinuous hand. "To tell you the truth, I lack all the materials to give you an absolutely perfect chance of immortality."

"So even if I asked you, you could not do it?"

"Oh, yes. I could make you immortal after a fashion, but I would not guarantee you a normal life."

"Could you get the materials you need?"

"There is a chance, yes." Orlando Sharvis seemed to consider carefully. "I see from your thoughts that you are torn between seeking immortality for yourself and asking me to 'cure' humanity in general. I doubt my ability to do the latter. I am not omnipotent, Clovis Marca. Besides, what if most of the human race dies eventually? There are others who will never die living here, inside the moon."

"Freaks," said Marca without thinking.

"You fear the end of the 'normal' human race, is that it?"

"Yes."

"I can't appreciate your fears, I'm afraid. However, I will think about this. Meanwhile I should tell you that enemies of yours seem to be everywhere at the moment, both within the moon and on its surface."

"What enemies?"

"Take for one. He is your enemy, though he thought himself your friend . . ."

"I have always known that much."

"And Andros Almer and his gang are currently running about all over the surface trying to find you. They have your woman—Fastina—with them."

"Is she safe?"

"Extremely. I take it that Almer regards the girl as his chief piece in the game he is playing with you . . ."

"Not a game I have any willing part in. How did he get to the moon? Why hasn't he discovered your tunnel?"

"I gather that his men's air cars all have tracer devices planted in them. This is to guard against them making any move that is contrary to what Almer wants them to do. Almer became suspicious after his scout had been gone longer than he expected. He traced the air car to your tower. He found Fastina there and you gone. He seized her and discovered that his air car had disappeared into the light region. It did not take him long to equip an expedition and come in search of you. The air car was traced to the moon, but now they are puzzled. I have sealed off and disguised my tunnel. Almer's instruments show that your air car is deep within the moon—but he cannot discover how it got there." Sharvis laughed softly. "He is extremely

137

perplexed. They have begun boring into the moon, but have managed to damage their instruments in one way o[r] another. I shall have to think of a way of dealing wit[h] them soon. They are threatening my privacy."

"You'll make sure Fastina's safe. She's innocent . . ."

"There was never a woman so innocent, I agree. Yes, [I] will make sure she is safe. I was not planning any sort o[f] spectacular destruction of Almer and his crew, Clovi[s] Marca. No. I am subtler than that, I hope."

"And what of Take?"

"Actually he is outside my laboratories now. He ha[s] been trying to get in for ten days without my noticing. [I] don't know what he wants here. He knows that he is fre[e] to come and go as he pleases, but he is a narrow[,] suspicious man. I expect we shall see him soon."

Sharvis turned gracefully. "I will leave you now, if yo[u] will excuse me. I have more than your particular proble[m] on my mind. Go where you will—you may find my hom[e] interesting."

Apparently without the aid of any mechanical device[,] Sharvis began to drift towards the flickering wall and sin[k] into it until he disappeared.

Marca began to see that Take had been wrong, after al[l,] in attributing malice to Sharvis's actions. The scientist'[s] actions were neither good nor bad as he had said. It wa[s] what one made of them that counted.

CHAPTER FIVE

The Truth

Orlando Sharvis's vast network of laboratories impressed Clovis Marca as he wandered around them in the days that followed. Marca had seen similar places on daylight Earth, but none so spectacular. Orlando Sharvis's laboratories had been designed not simply for function, but also for beauty. The complex building, carved from the interior of mountains Sharvis had himself created, had been built by Sharvis alone. It was difficult to realise this as he explored room after room, passage after passage.

The laboratories were only part of the system. Some rooms seemed to have been designed merely as rooms, with no other purpose than to exist for their own sake. The building was, in fact, a palace of incredible beauty. There were galleries and chambers in it which, in their sweeping architecture and colours, were unmatched by anything in the history of the world. Clovis Marca was moved profoundly, and he felt that no one capable of such work could be evil.

In one very large chamber he found several works that were not by Sharvis. They were unmistakably by Alodios.

Marca went to look for Sharvis and found the self-deformed giant at last, sitting thoughtfully in a chair in a room that swirled with soft, dark colours. He asked Sharvis about Alodios's work.

"Normally," Sharvis told him, "I ask no price for my gifts—but Alodios insisted. He was the only modern artist I admired, so I was pleased to accept them. I hope you en-

139

joy them. I hope that someday others will come to see them."

"You would welcome visitors, then?"

"Particularly men and women of taste and intellect, yes. Alodios was with me for some time here. I enjoyed our talks very much."

Memory of Alodios's trapped, tormented eyes returned to Marca, and he felt troubled.

Sharvis's shrivelled mouth smiled as if in sadness. "I can refuse no one, Marca. In many ways I would have enjoyed Alodios's company, but, in the end, I had to do what he demanded of me. I fear that you will not stay long, for one reason or another."

Still confused, Marca left the room.

Sharvis's palace was timeless. There were no chronometers to tell Marca how long he had been there, but it was probably a day or two later that the scientist sought Marca out as he listened to the singing words of the mobiles in the Alodios chamber.

"You must hate me for interrupting," whispered Sharvis, "but our friend Take has arrived at last. He finally took the simple way in and entered by the main door. I am glad he has arrived, for I wanted to speak to you both together. I will leave you to finish the novel if you like . . ."

Marca glanced up at the red and pink mottled face that seemed to look at him anxiously, although it was impossible to tell from the faceted eyes what Sharvis's feelings were.

"No. I'll come," said Marca getting up.

Leaving the novel, Marca went with Orlando Sharvis to the room of flame where they had first confronted each other.

Take was there, standing in the middle of the room, the coloured shadows playing across his face. He had his hands clasped behind his back and there was a defeated look about him.

He raised his strange head and nodded to Marca.

"I should have battered your skull to pulp and taken your corpse with me," he said. "I'm sorry, Clovis Marca."

Marca felt disturbed and hostile as he confronted the man who had twice tried to murder him. "I think you're misguided, Take. I've been talking to Orlando Sharvis and . . ."

"And you are as gullible as all the others. I told you that you would be. He has deadened your brain. What have you said to him, Orlando?"

The giant spread his sinuous hands. "I have only answered his questions truthfully, Ezek."

"Glibly, you mean. Your truth and mine are very different!"

Marca began to feel sorry for Take. "What Sharvis says is correct." he said. "He has been fair with me. He hasn't lied. He hasn't tried to encourage me to do anything I do not want to do. In fact, to some degree, he has tried to discourage me."

"To some degree?" Take's deep voice rose until it bore a hint of despair. "You fool, Clovis Marca, I wasted my time when I tried to protect you."

"I told you—I am my own man. I need no protection."

"You are no longer your own man, whether you realise it now or not. Already you are Sharvis's—you cretin!"

"Please, Ezek, this is unworthy of you," Sharvis interrupted, gliding forward. "When have I ever tried to exert my will on others—at least since the Titan failure? Have I ever tricked you, Ezek? I have always been straightforward with you."

"You devious man—you destroyed me!"

"In those early days I was still learning. You wanted what I could give you. Why blame me for my ignorance? These outbursts only do you discredit."

"You were never ignorant. You were born with knowledge—and it made you the evil monstrosity . . ."

"Take!" Marca put his hand on the man's arm. "He has a point."

"You know nothing of all this, of all he has done. Not only to me, but to all who have ever had any dealings with him. He is subtle, persuasive and malevolent. Do not believe anything he tells you. He gave me immortality, but he robbed me of my ability to appreciate life. Happiness and love are denied me. There is only one thing that moves me now—and that is suffering. I am dead, but he won't give me proper death. All his 'gifts' are like that—all are flawed. He pretends to exert no power over you—and you find yourself a creation of his warped need to make others like himself!"

"You want me to kill you, Ezek?" Sharvis said. "Is that it? You must understand what that implies. Death. It is final. I could not revive you."

"Now you are trying to raise my hope," Take said, turning away. "Then you will say you have not the conscience to kill me."

"It depends . . ." Sharvis mused. "It depends on Clovis Marca's decision." Before Marca could ask what he meant, he continued, "Almer and your woman, Fastina, are here."

"Here? How did they get here?"

"Almer had Fastina Cahmin with him in his air car as he went on yet another circuit of the area of the moon above the ice. I had waited for this to happen, as it had to eventually. I opened the tunnel a little way. Almer entered to investigate. I closed the tunnel. Almer came here. It was the only way he could go. After that, my robots escorted them to my laboratories. They are at the entrance now."

"And his men are still outside?"

"Yes. I was forced to remove all sources of heat from the area. They are not dead—merely in suspended animation of sorts."

"Frozen?" Marca asked.

"In a way. Now, you must tell me what you want me to do with Almer and the girl. Do you want to see them?"

"Almer might try something violent . . ."

Sharvis chuckled. "He could try all he wanted, but I doubt if he could do much damage here."

"I would like to see Fastina. I would like to ask what she thinks of my accepting immortality from you. And there's one other thing I would like to ask you . . ."

"What's that?"

"Could you give her immortality as well?"

142

"I could give you both immortality, yes—with the materials I have at hand now."

"You have got hold of them."

"I might have done, yes."

Marca could not puzzle out exactly what Sharvis meant. He turned to Take. "You've spoken very melodramatically just recently, Take. Do you really want death?"

Take still had his back to them. "Ask Sharvis how many times I have begged him to destroy me properly," he said.

Sharvis pursed his shrivelled lips. "Who knows?" he said. "Perhaps everyone's wish can be made to come true today. I will go and fetch the new arrivals."

Sharvis glided into the wall and disappeared. Take turned back to face Marca. "Come to your senses while you have time," he said urgently. "Leave with Fastina. I will deal with Almer, if Sharvis does not. You will be free."

Marca shook his head impatiently. "Sharvis is obviously not normal in any way," he said, "but I am sure your judgement of him is biased . . ."

"Of course it is—by all I've seen. He is wiser than any man has ever been. He knows how to trick someone of your intelligence. He means you nothing but harm. If he gives you immortality as he gave it to me, you will feel nothing except despair—*eternally*. Don't you realise that?"

"Surely your emotions are only dead because you have refused to awaken them?" Marca said. "Have you never thought that the fault lies with you and not with Sharvis?"

"Your mind has already been turned by his logic," Take said. "I have tried to save you from an eternity of misery. You will not listen. I'll say no more."

"Misery for you? It need not be for me. Besides, I have not decided yet."

"You decided the first day you heard of Orlando Sharvis. Don't deceive yourself, Clovis Marca."

Sharvis came back through the walls of flame. Behind him, looking about him warily, stepped Almer and behind Almer came a pale-faced Fastina.

Almer still wore his heavy black hooded cloak and mask. There was still a sword at his side. He was still arrogant in his manner, though his arrogance was now plainly inspired by fear.

"What is this place?" he asked as soon as he saw Marca. "Who is this creature?"

Fastina moved uncertainly towards Marca, her expression changing from despair to relief. "Oh, Clovis!"

He took her in his arms and kissed her as she trembled there.

"Whatever happens, we are safe together now," he assured her. "I'm sorry I left you as I did—but I had to. And it was for the best, as you'll find out."

She looked up at him. There were tears in her deep blue eyes. "Are you sure?"

"I'm sure."

Almer pointed a gloved finger at Sharvis. "I warn you, whoever you are—I rule Earth, even the nightside. I have an army at my command . . ."

Sharvis smiled. "I have offered you no harm, I believe, Andros Almer. I see from your mind that you are afraid; that you are afraid of your own weakness more than anything else. I will do nothing to you. All who visit me are welcome. All who ask something of me are granted it. Take off your armour. Relax."

Almer dropped his hand to his sword-hilt and turned to Marca.

"Is he some ally of yours, Marca?"

"He's no one's ally," Marca told him. "Do as he says. Relax."

"That world out there," Almer walked to a couch and ostentatiously leaned back on it. "How was it created? I never heard . . ."

"Orlando Sharvis created it," Marca told him.

Almer looked at the giant with the pink and red mottled skin and the expressionless, faceted eyes. "You are Orlando Sharvis? The scientist? I thought you were dead. What happened to you? How did you become like that?"

Sharvis shrugged. "Clovis Marca will answer your questions. I must leave for a while."

When Sharvis had gone, Marca explained everything to Almer and Fastina. As he finished, Almer said: "He's neutral, you say. He'll do anything for anyone who asks?"

"Anything within his power."

In the shadows Take stirred. "You deserve a gift from Sharvis, Almer," he said.

"What does he mean?" Almer asked.

"He's demented—he has an old grudge against Sharvis," Marca told him. He now realised that Sharvis was indeed neutral. If he granted a request from Almer, what would the consequences be?

Sharvis returned to the room of flame.

"Well, Ezek," he said to Take, "here is what I can do. I can use certain elements in your body to give Clovis Marca immortality. It will mean, of course, that I shall have to destroy you. So there it is—his immortality for your life, and everyone gets what they want."

"I haven't yet said I want immortality," Marca said, "unless Fastina can have it too."

"I promised you both immortality," Sharvis reminded him.

"What do you say, Fastina?" Marca asked her.

"Would you want me for all that time?"

"Shall we accept Sharvis's gift and become immortal?" She hesitated. Then she whispered: "Yes."

Sharvis looked at Take. "What do you say, Ezek? Marca's immortality for your life?"

Take shook his head. "Another of your jokes, Orlando. You know I would not do that . . ."

Marca broke in. "I thought so. You have talked about the horror of immortality, but, now it comes to it, you want to keep your life, after all. Very well."

Take moved into the centre of the room and grasped Marca by the shoulder. "You were once admired for your intelligence, Clovis Marca—look what you have become. Selfish and stupid! My desire for death probably far outweighs your desire for immortality. You have missed the subtlety of Orlando's bargain."

"And what would that be?"

"He knows that I have tried to prevent you from doing

145

something that will cause you terrible misery, that I would have no other human being suffer what I suffer. I sought only to prevent that suffering in you. Now he offers me peace at the price of letting you become what I am. Do you see now?"

"I think you are over-complicating the matter," Marca said coolly. "I will have immortality. I will make use of it, if you dare not!"

Take moved away again, towards the shifting wall. The dancing shadows seemed to give his face an expression of anguish.

"Very well," he said quietly. "Take it and hope that one day Orlando Sharvis makes you the offer he has made me!"

Concentrating on this argument no one had noticed Andros Almer draw his sword and stalk towards Orlando Sharvis to press the tip against the scientist's great chest.

Sharvis was not surprised. It was evident that he had read Almer's mind before the man crossed the room.

He reached forward, displaying the same rapid reflexes as Take, and snatched the sword from Almer's hand. He snapped the sword in two and then into four and dropped the pieces casually in front of the astonished man.

"What did you intend to do?" Sharvis asked gently.

"I intended to force you to release me."

"Why?"

"Because you are in league with Marca."

"I have told you, and he has told you, that I am in league with no one. I merely do what I am asked, if I can."

"Could you turn the world again?" Almer asked suddenly.

Sharvis smiled thoughtfully. "Is that what you want me to do? I see from your mind that you would claim credit for the action, that you think it would give you an advantage to seem some sort of miracle worker. You are full of superstition, aren't you?"

"Could you turn the world? Have you that power?"

"You think if I did it would give you mastery over it all, don't you?"

146

"I think it would. I would be able to control it all, then. I would leave you in peace. It would not be in my interest to reveal your presence in the world."

Orlando Sharvis looked down at Almer and smiled again.

"Would you interfere with Clovis Marca and Fastina Cahmin?"

"No. I swear. Give me the opportunity—and I will do the rest."

"I have had a project ready for some time," Sharvis said. "It is as yet untested. Since the raid I have been fascinated by the space-dwellers and the forces they commanded. I have discovered something of their secret. I might be able to do it."

"Try!" Almer said eagerly. "I will give you anything in return."

Sharvis shook his head. "I ask no price for my gifts and services. We shall see what we can do when we have settled Clovis Marca's problem." He glanced at Marca, Fastina and Take.

"You are sure you are willing to make this sacrifice Ezek?"

"It is no sacrifice. Marca will be the sufferer, not I."

"And you two—Marca? Fastina?"

"I'm ready," Marca said.

Fastina nodded hesitantly.

"Then we can begin at once," said Sharvis, with a trace of eagerness. "You will wait here, Almer, and we will discuss your request later. Go where you like in my laboratories. I will seek you out when I have finished."

Take, Marca and Fastina followed him through the wall of flame and into an arched corridor.

"I have already prepared my equipment," he told them. "The operation itself will not take too long."

Fastina gripped Marca's hand and trembled, but she said nothing.

· CHAPTER SIX

The Turn

When Marca eventually awoke it was with a feeling of increased numbness through his body, as if he were paralysed. But when he tried to move his limbs, he found that they responded perfectly. He smiled up at Orlando Sharvis who was looking down at him. Behind Sharvis were the blank cabinets in which his equipment was housed.

"Thank you," Marca said. "Is it done?"

"It is. Poor Ezek's few remains were flushed away a couple of hours ago. It was a pity that that was the only way."

"And Fastina?"

"She, too has been operated on. With her it was an altogether easier job. She is perfectly well as you will see when you join her."

"Were there any difficulties in my operation?"

"There could be some side effects. We shall have to see. Come, we'll go to find Fastina."

Fastina was in the Alodios room. The novel was in progress, with abstract colours and delicate music mingling with the voice of Alodios himself narrating the prose sequences. She turned it off and ran towards him, her face alight with pleasure. She looked now as she had first looked when they had met on his return to daylight Earth. He felt something like pleasure, himself, as he reached out with his insensitive fingers and took her hands.

"Oh," she said, "you *are* all right. I wasn't sure . . ." She

148

glanced at the scientist. "Did Orlando Sharvis tell you the good news? He didn't tell me until after the operation!"

"What's that?"

"I can have children. My ovaries weren't badly affected by the omega radiation. He was able to make them healthy again. That's what he meant by immortality. He is a good man, after all!"

Marca was puzzled. "But you alone being able to bear children isn't enough . . ."

"You, too, are now capable of fathering children," Orlando told him. "I hope you call your first son Orlando."

Marca did not feel the emotion he expected. He tried to smile at Fastina, but it was difficult. He had to make his lips move in a smile. She looked at him in alarm. "What's wrong, Clovis?"

"I don't know." His voice now sounded just a little flat. Behind them there was a rustle of cloth as Sharvis folded his strange arms.

"I'm feeling numb, that's all," he said. "The operation did it. It will wear off soon, won't it, Sharvis?"

Sharvis shook his mottled head. "I'm afraid not. That was the side effect I mentioned. In using various glands and organs extracted from Take, I somehow made the same mistake I made on him. You will not be able to feel anything very strongly, Clovis Marca. I'm sorry."

"You knew this would happen!" He turned on the scientist. "You knew! Take was right!"

"Nonsense. You will get used to it. I have."

"You are like this all the time?"

"Exactly. I have been for centuries. Mental sensations soon replace the physical kind. I find much that is stimulating still." Sharvis smiled. "What you have lost will be made up for by what you have gained."

"Damiago was right. You give and take away at the same time. I should have listened to Take." Marca struck at his body and felt nothing. He bit his tongue and there was only a little pain.

"I must live forever like this?" he said. "It defeats the whole thing."

149

"You knew the dangers. Take told you of them. But Take was weak. You are strong. Besides, you can now have children."

"How, when I feel nothing?"

"I have done my best. I have seen to it that certain stimuli will have certain effects."

Marca nodded despairingly and looked at Fastina.

"I still love you, Clovis," she said. "I'll stay with you."

"It would be wise," Sharvis agreed, "if you wish to continue your race. Clovis Marca I have given you both the things you asked of me."

"I suppose so," said Marca. "It is a sacrifice I should be proud to make. But I wish I had known I was to sacrifice something . . ."

"An unknowing martyr is no martyr at all," Sharvis agreed. "For your own sake, I would not make you that."

"Are you so neutral?" Marca said. "Are you not simply a complicated mixture of good and evil?"

Sharvis laughed. "You describe me as if I were an ordinary man. I assure you, I am entirely neutral."

"You have forced this girl to live with a man who cannot respond to her, cannot love her except in a strange way—a way he cannot demonstrate . . ."

"I have forced her to do no such thing. She is free to do as she wishes. She will bear you children—that is her immortality. You will live on. Her life will be short enough . . ."

"Am I invulnerable—like Take?"

"That happened, yes, in the transference of Take's parts to your body."

"I see." Marca sighed. "What do we do now?"

"You are free to leave. However, if you wish to stay and see me try to answer Almer's request . . ."

"You can do it? You can make the world turn?"

"I think so. Do you want to come with me, back to the flame room?"

They went with him to the flame room and found Almer there. He looked as if he had not moved since they left him.

"Why didn't you do as I suggested?" Sharvis asked him.

"You could have seen everything there is to see in my laboratories."

"I didn't trust you," Almer mumbled. "Are those two immortal now? They don't look any different."

"He's sulking, Clovis," said Fastina with a smile. In spite of what had happened to her lover, she seemed elated still.

"They are," Sharvis told Almer.

"I'm hungry," Almer said.

"I've been a poor host. Let's go and have something to eat."

After they had eaten, Sharvis led them through a door and down to a hall which was empty save for two bronze air cars covered in baroque decoration. They climbed in to one.

They began to descend through a tunnel narrower than the one which led into the hollow world of the moon, but which wound downwards at a much greater incline. The air became thick and salty. The tunnel was lit by dim strips in its sides and they felt the blood pound in their ears as the pressure increased.

"We are just about to reach the level of the ocean bottom," Sharvis told them. "This tunnel leads from the moon to the rock below it." He continued to talk, but Marca could hear very little but the booming in his eardrums. Sharvis seemed to be explaining how he had managed to build the tunnel.

At last they left the tunnel and entered a huge, dark cavern. Sharvis guided the air car to the side and turned on the lights.

Water seeped down all the walls of the great grotto. The place seemed of natural origin. On its floor stood a machine.

The machine was large and had been coated in some kind of yellow protective plastic. In its centre was a gigantic power unit. From this led a structure of rigid pipes and cables attached to a grid which encircled the whole apparatus.

"As you can imagine," Sharvis's voice said over the

151

pounding heartbeats that filled Marca's ears, "I have had no chance to test this device. The model seemed to work successfully enough, but I was never sure that the power was sufficient to do the job. The thing is, in effect, an engine which will push in a given direction. It will, with luck, begin to turn the world sufficiently rapidly to restore the planet's momentum."

Sharvis took the air car down to the slimy floor of the cavern and stepped out of it, gliding across to the machine. "The only control is on the machine itself. I thought it unwise to risk connecting another control that could be operated from my laboratories. I only invent, as I told you. I never use my inventions for any specific purpose unless asked to do so. I am grateful for the opportunity you have given me, Andros Almer."

Dimly, Marca saw Almer huddled in his cloak, his hood drawn about his face. The man seemed to be watching Sharvis intently as the scientist stepped over to the machine and, after hesitating for a moment, depressed a stud on the small control panel.

Nothing happened.

Sharvis came back to the air car and clambered in, his huge bulk dominating them.

"It has a timing mechanism so that we can return without undue haste to my laboratories." He turned the air car back into the tunnel.

Later, they sat looking up at the huge screen, which showed a view of the Earth from above, evidently transmitted from an old weather control satellite.

Sharvis swung a chronometer from a hidden panel below the screen, watching closely as the seconds indicator swept around it.

A faint tremor began to be sensed in the room.

"It will be gradual," Sharvis told them. "It will take quite a few hours. This is to ensure that no major upheavals take place on the planet. The whole operation should be quite smooth, if I have judged correctly."

The laboratory shook violently for a few seconds and then subsided.

The picture on the screen showed the day side of Earth. They could see no indication of movement as yet.

"Of course," Sharvis said casually, "There is just a chance that the engine will begin to push in another direction and carry the Earth out of her normal orbit. I hope it is not towards the sun." He chuckled.

"It's moving," whispered Fastina.

It was moving. A shadow was beginning to inch across the outline of Asia.

The laboratory trembled, but this time the vibration was steady.

They watched in silence as the shadow lengthened over Asia and touched Africa. The coastline of South America came into view.

As the hours passed and the vibration in the laboratory became familiar, the shadow reached Europe and spread into the Atlantic.

Later they saw the whole of the American continent appear. The vibrations increased, as if the engine were labouring.

Sharvis looked calmly at the instruments below the screen.

They could now see the blinding whiteness of the ice-covered Pacific and then they could make out the visible surface of the moon rising from the ice in clear daylight.

The vibrations increased. The laboratory rocked. They were flung to the floor and the picture above them wavered and then became steady again.

From far below them they heard a deep, echoing sound and again the laboratory shook.

Then everything was still.

They looked at one another and at the screen.

The world had stopped turning.

Almer turned to Sharvis. "What's happened? Start the thing up again."

Sharvis chuckled. "Well, well. I've turned the world for you, Andros Almer. But the engine must have reversed its thrust . . ."

"Keep it turning!" Almer bellowed.

"I'm not sure that I can. Come, we'll investigate."

They followed him as he glided from the laboratory and back to the place where the air cars were.

Again they flew down the tunnel, through the moon and beneath it through the ocean floor until they entered the cave.

The air was scorching hot and there was no longer any moisture on the grotto walls.

They saw the machine. It was now merely a fused tangle of blackened metal.

"Overloaded," Sharvis shouted, and began to laugh.

"You expected this?" Almer called over the roar of his own heartbeats. "Did you?"

Sharvis looked around. "We'd better leave immediately. The section joining the tunnel from the moon to the bed of the sea has been weakened. You can imagine the pressure outside it. If we don't go, we'll be crushed or drowned."

Almer stood up in the air car. "You did this deliberately! You knew the machine was incapable of turning the Earth!"

Sharvis swung the air car into the tunnel. Water was already running in a steady river down its sides.

Almer beat at Sharvis's heavy body, but the scientist continued to chuckle while he guided the air car upwards.

Marca and Fastina clung together as Sharvis increased the speed. There was a strange creaking noise filling the tunnel now.

Eventually they returned to the chamber below the laboratories and Sharvis hurried to the door, with Almer still clinging to him and repeating again and again, "Did you? Did you? Did you?"

Sharvis ignored Almer and entered another room. The wall slid back at his touch and he began to run his seemingly boneless fingers over a console, his eyes on the indicators above. Again the room trembled slightly.

A little later he stepped back.

"I've sealed off the tunnel," he said. "There'll be no trouble there."

Sharvis seemed to be relieved. He turned his pink and red mottled face towards Marca and Fastina and regarded them with his expressionless, faceted eyes.

Almer appeared to have exhausted himself. He lay against a wall mumbling.

"Did you know the engine could not work properly?" Fastina asked Sharvis innocently.

"I have given Almer what he really wanted, I'm sure," Sharvis replied enigmatically. "He wanted the world turned. I turned it. Now his empire lies in the night. Could that be where it belongs?"

"The people," Fastina said. "The ordinary people . . ."

"Those who wish to escape him may now do so. But few will, I think. The darkness is safe. They can huddle in it until death comes. Isn't that what they want? Haven't I given everyone what they really wish?"

Marca looked at him unemotionally. "Certainly the darkness mirrors the darkness in their minds," he said. "But do they deserve it?"

"Who is to say?" shrugged Sharvis.

Almer stepped forward. "I wish to go home," he said levelly. Apparently he had recovered and had accepted what had happened. It seemed strange to Marca that he should do so with such apparent equanimity.

"You may do as you please," said Sharvis with a trace of malicious humour. It was almost as if he felt he had paid Almer back for the pitiful attempt the man had made on his life. "Will you find your own way out?"

Almer marched from the room. "I have found it, thanks to you," he called as he left.

"And what of you, Clovis Marca?" asked Sharvis. "What will you do now?"

"We will return to my father's tower," Marca said stiffly.

"And raise your children?" Sharvis said. "I trust you will think in time that your sacrifice was worthwhile."

"Maybe." Marca glanced sadly at Fastina. "But will you think the same, Fastina?"

She shook her head. "I don't know, Clovis."

Marca looked suddenly up at Sharvis. "I have just realised," he said. "You have played another joke on us, I believe."

"No," said Sharvis, reading his mind. "The radiation

still exists, certainly. But your children's life cycle will be shorter since you will now lack the means to induce longevity. They will have time to adapt and reproduce. And I have made sure that you will never be affected by the radiation. Doubtless you will help father your children's children. It appears to be an established tradition in your family already."

Fastina took Marca's arm. "Let's go, Clovis," she said. "Back to the tower."

"If it means anything," Sharvis told them as they left, "something has changed which might give you encouragement. It is a sentimental thing to say, I know . . ."

"What's that?" said Fastina, looking back at him.

"You once faced the evening. Now you face the morning. I wish you and your offspring well. Perhaps I will come to see them sometime, or you will send them to see me?"

Even then, as he walked away from the strange scientist, Marca was still unsure if Sharvis was moved by malice or charity, or whether the neutrality he claimed was founded on some deep understanding of life which was available only to him.

EPILOGUE

The tower now existed in the dawn, but the quality of the light had not altered. The red dust continued to blow and the brown lichen grew around the base of the tower.

The tower's shadow lay behind it now, and the shadow never moved. One day Fastina told Clovis Marca that she was pregnant.

"Good," he said as he sat immobile by the window watching the distant sun on the horizon, and Fastina put her arms around his neck and kissed his cold face and stroked his unresponsive body, and loved him with a love that now had pity in it.

Mechanically, he reached up with one of his numb hands and touched her arm and continued to stare out at the sun and thought about Orlando Sharvis, wondering still whether the scientist had acted from good intentions or evil, or neither; wondering about himself and what he was; wondering why his wife cried so silently; wondering vaguely why he could not and never would cry with her. He wanted nothing, regretted nothing; feared nothing.

(Please turn page)